MOUNTAIN LOVE

Ria Williams is part of an agency with an assignment to take pictures in western Norway for a travel brochure. There is one problem — she is frightened of heights. Karl Vigeland, a strong-minded Norwegian, owns the travel company and a love/hate relationship develops between them. After Karl rescues Ria when her car breaks down on a mountain road, their problems are resolved.

SHEILA BENTON

◆

MOUNTAIN LOVE

Complete and Unabridged

LINFORD
Leicester

First published in Great Britain in 2003

First Linford Edition
published 2004

British Library CIP Data

Benton, Sheila
    Mountain love.—Large print ed.—
Linford romance library
1. Love stories
2. Large type books
I. Title
823.9′2 [F]

ISBN 1–84395–449–4

Published by
F. A. Thorpe (Publishing)
Anstey, Leicestershire

Set by Words & Graphics Ltd.
Anstey, Leicestershire
Printed and bound in Great Britain by
T. J. International Ltd., Padstow, Cornwall

This book is printed on acid-free paper

TO THE MEMORY OF JUSTIN

1

Although not handsome, he was the most arresting man Ria Williams had ever seen. Brilliant blue eyes under heavy brows held her stare until her glance went to the wide shoulders in the thick, Norwegian sweater.

'Some man,' she breathed silently.

He shifted slightly, breaking the spell, and her eyes flew up to meet his amused expression. She bit her lip like a small girl caught spying on a grown-up party. Turning away she shook the auburn waves of hair forward to hide her burning face, wishing she had held his look instead of dropping her eyes in such a ridiculously embarrassed fashion.

She was furious to be caught staring as though she'd never seen a man before. Tossing back her hair she gripped the rail of the boat and tried to put him out of her mind, but from the centre of her back spread an exciting, shivery sensation as though someone's eyes were upon her.

There was no reason to assume that he was still looking but the intensity of his inspection had rocked her composure. But then, she grinned to herself, trying to get the tiny incident into proportion, I inspected him as well and he was certainly worth it.

I'm supposed to be a liberated woman, she thought wryly, but put me in front of anything as male as that man and I crumble. I certainly won't want to see him around once we dock, far too distracting. Anyway, she doubted he would be in the same type of accommodation as her. There was an air of confidence about him clearly saying he was used to the best of everything. She also thought he could be going home to a wife and family or to some gorgeous girl friend.

She fervently hoped he was a native and wouldn't be doing the tourist bit like her for she could well do without any outside disturbance for the next few weeks. All her attention was needed for the job. The opportunity had fallen into her lap and she was determined to take full advantage of her luck.

Knowing she needed to concentrate on work she fingered the camera slung round her neck. Her eye was caught by an isolated farmhouse and she started to focus, trying to capture the loneliness of the spot. Soon she'd forgotten the man as she gazed upwards to the mighty granite mountain, its lower slopes covered in pines while snow, white and silent, clung to the top.

Ria had never seen anything as truly magnificent as the scenery closing around her. The last of the sun played on the ripples left by the white ferry as it disturbed the still, quiet waters of the Norwegian fiord. Kneeling at her bag she quickly changed the film knowing that it would be easy to get really striking pictures if this was a sample of what she would see during the next few weeks. The weather was the only thing that worried her. It was nearly at the end of the summer and winter came early in this part of the world.

She brushed off the knees of her jeans as she straightened up.

'Over there,' his voice came, deep and deliberate. 'Look there.'

Startled, she relaxed her hold and allowed the camera to swing loose from its strap. Some sixth sense told her that it was the man she had been staring at earlier.

'Don't miss it. We'll soon be too far along.'

Ria looked up a long way at the man who was standing close to her. He placed one hand on her shoulder, turning her slightly.

'That's what you should be taking.'

He pointed at the narrow inlet where the deep waters reflected the sweep of the slopes on either side. She caught her breath, partly at his touch and partly at the beauty mirrored in the depths, and shaking off the hand she raised her camera again. Sighing in satisfaction she turned to thank him but the man had disappeared.

Funny, she thought, I could have sworn he was a native but that English was practically without an accent, just a bit deliberate. I wonder what nationality he is. Twisting right around she risked a look but there was no sign of the large man in the thick sweater. It occurred to her then that she had not spoken a word but had simply done as he'd instructed. Such had been the strength of his personality.

Watching the almost awesome panorama as the ferry continued its journey, she worried about the task ahead. Her career as a photographer for Worldwide Journeys depended on this assignment. Frowning, she thought, not for the first time, that perhaps she wasn't mentally ready for a big assignment like this. But the flu virus John caught had postponed the job once and then was further complicated by him catching chickenpox from his sister's children.

After that, there was no-one to send but his assistant, Ria. At one point it was suggested they look outside the agency to find another, more experienced photographer but the ever-constant threat of an early winter made it impossible to arrange in time. So she had packed her things, closed her tiny flat and taken John's place.

It was a challenge she accepted having no doubts about her technical ability. The country was rugged and even primitive in parts but that didn't worry her. The roads were a different matter. Her skin prickled with cold knowing she'd never had a good head for heights and to drive the mountainous hairpins alone was a frightening prospect.

She squared her shoulders, telling herself that it was just a question of thinking it through logically, a typical case of mind over matter which was no problem for a strong-minded, young woman with a lot to gain.

Earlier that day, she'd picked up a hire car at Bergen. Then with the help of a map she had driven nearly two hundred miles to the ferry which would take her to the cabin site where she would stay until the project was complete. The drive had been exhausting and difficult. The road wound through a series of long, dark tunnels through the mountains which strained her eyes and slowed her down considerably.

Watching the little landing stage come nearer she decided to go down to the lower deck and sit in her car. She thought how different it was to the large sea ferries with their booming Tannoy instructions. This was very relaxed. Probably nobody would have worried if she'd stayed in her vehicle the whole journey and slept.

The ferry bumped to a stop and the first car drove off — and what a car. It was of Ria's dreams, a sleek red Porsche. She watched it so longingly she slowed the smooth line of cars rolling off and had to quickly switch on her engine to the grins and laughter of the crew. Ria grinned back and gave them a wave thinking how different they were to the large, grim man who had spoken to her a short time ago.

An hour later, she found the site and checked in. She was taking the key from the young blonde receptionist when it nearly fell from her hand as she was startled by loud and insistent hooting. The honey-skinned girl was quite undisturbed and just lifted her eyebrows slightly as she smiled.

'Is that your small blue car?' she asked Ria.

'Er . . . yes,' Ria answered.

'I think you are in the way of the Porsche.'

Ria glanced out thinking what a coincidence that the car she'd watched so jealously was also staying here.

'What an impatient man. I've only been a moment. Oh, well,' she said with a shrug, 'I'm going to my cabin now anyway. It's been a long day.'

8

The girl smiled sympathetically but then her expression changed as Ria took her time gathering up some brochures from the counter.

'I don't think you should keep him waiting,' she said uneasily.

'Why not? He might have guessed another visitor would have to park in front of him. He didn't exactly leave room for someone to go alongside. He was most inconsiderate. I hope there won't be many like him staying here.'

'Oh, he's not a visitor. He is the owner.'

Ria stopped in her tracks, her temper rising.

'Owner or not, I think he's a very bad-mannered man.'

She took her time fastening her shoulder-bag and adjusting the strap comfortably. The blonde girl looked alarmed at her casual manner and Ria wondered if all the women here were as subservient as the receptionist.

'That kind of attitude doesn't suit me,' she muttered to herself and was half inclined to look around the room at the posters on the walls that advertised various trips and keep the bad-tempered man waiting even longer. Then seeing how agitated the other girl had become she decided to look tomorrow and gathered up the rest of her things.

A loud tattoo on the horn started again and drawing herself up to her full height she marched through the door, straight past the Porsche and slid into her small car. A quick glance in the mirror gave her a view of a half-turned head of tawny-coloured hair above a patterned sweater.

Noting with satisfaction that the Porsche was signalling right to go back to the road, she started to swing the car to the left and her temper soon disappeared as she wound her way up to the cabins. Built from Norwegian pine, they stood on terraces, each with a covered porch and a grass-topped roof. Parking in the neat little space in front of Number 32 she grabbed her precious bag of cameras and lenses and climbed the two steps to the door.

Warm and mellow from floor to ceiling were narrow wooden planks lining the walls. Colourful Scandinavian rugs hung like huge posters cheerfully around the well-furnished living-room from which a small kitchen area was sectioned off. A bedroom with twin beds, a smaller room and a bathroom completed her living quarters. Coming back to the main room she investigated the cast-iron, wood-burning stove in the corner of the main room and realised why there had been a box of wood by the side of the cabin. She could even have cosy evenings by her own fire.

Standing alone in the centre of the room she hugged herself as she looked round. It was all hers, perfect and private, until her task was completed. Here, there was peace and comfort and lots of time to plan the job. Sighing in satisfaction, she flopped on to the couch. The little home was perfect and she had everything she wanted. The scenery was out of this world and the atmosphere was stimulating. With a mounting excitement she knew that she must do her very best work here and the future stretched in front of her, successful and secure.

Later, when she had brought in the rest of her luggage including a box of provisions, she relaxed, curling her hands around a mug of coffee. Sniffing the strong brew appreciatively she watched the steam drifting upwards and drew her bare feet up under the edge of her long blue towelling robe.

The unpolished table in front of her was covered with brochures and information for the assignment. A copy of the letter from the owner of the tour company was on top of the pile. It was precise and to the point. He wanted the best and had asked for their most experienced operator. Ria gulped, feeling suddenly agitated. She wasn't exactly experienced but she knew she was good.

Everyone said she had talent and this could be the break she needed and nothing was going to stop her doing her most brilliant work. The signature on the letter caught her eye. It was large in a bold black script. She peered closer and couldn't quite make out the scrawl but neatly typed beneath it was the name, Karl Vigeland.

Well, Karl Vigeland, she thought, you demanded the best and I'm going to give it to you.

Suddenly she was startled by the sounds of someone outside the cabin crunching the pine needles underfoot. As she listened, the sounds appeared to come nearer and she put the coffee down abruptly, spilling a few drops. She wasn't expecting visitors tonight and certainly wasn't dressed for them.

The footsteps stopped and she began to smile. No-one knew she was here yet. Whoever it was had probably walked on, but they hadn't, and she jumped violently, the smile leaving her face as she heard the loud knocking.

Reluctant to open the door, she stood up slowly, wondering if the neighbouring cabin was occupied or if she was alone.

But perhaps it is just someone to welcome me, she tried to tell herself as she peered through the window into the dark night. Then, tying the belt of her soft robe more securely about her, she opened the door.

'You,' she whispered, but the man didn't hear her.

His frame filled the doorway and his expression told her that this was no welcoming call. She stood speechless and wished desperately that she was still dressed in her jeans. She looked beyond him to the empty, dark night and felt afraid. Then her usual commonsense came to her rescue and she raised her eyebrows in query, forcing him to speak first.

Ria tried to edge to one side so that she was half hidden by the door. She didn't attempt to speak.

'What are you doing here?' he

demanded eventually, one foot thrusting its way inside.

He was just too insolent and suddenly she felt her temper rising.

'What on earth are you doing bursting in here at this time of night?'

'I own this place and I do what I please. This cabin is supposed to be for the photographer from Worldwide Journeys, so what are you doing here?'

She grabbed the side of the door as shock caught up with her. This couldn't be happening. His form blurred and came back into focus as she shook her head. Then as though she was listening to someone else she heard her own voice reply.

'That's just who I am,' she said sweetly. 'If you'd just like to apologise and go, I'm sure we can both forget this incident.'

There was a long silence as he looked her over.

'I'm expecting a man.'

'Sorry to disappoint you but you may have noticed I'm a woman.'

His eyes surveyed arrogantly the auburn head and travelled down.

'I had noticed.'

Ria's mouth tightened at his chauvinistic inspection of her body.

'Well, now you've proved I'm a woman perhaps you'd like to get out of here. I've had a long day and I'm tired.'

He raised his eyebrows.

'Poor little woman's tired, is she? That's why I asked for a man. This isn't a job for a woman, especially an English woman.'

She threw back her head as her temper rose once more.

'Just what have you got against women and English women in particular?'

He spoke slowly, contrasting with her rather breathless tone.

'Oh, I like women,' he said and added insolently, 'in the right place, of course. But English women are useless. They have to be entertained and protected. I've seen them here, fluttering around complaining about the

16

roads and the lack of night life.'

Her fine skin paled.

'I've no time for so-called night life,' she replied, then her energy ebbed and she said wearily, 'Just what has this to do with you? I'm only answerable to the owner of Worldwide Journeys.'

Somehow they had moved into the room and she sank on to the couch. He glared down at her.

'I own Worldwide Journeys.'

Ria gasped and sank deeper into the couch. What on earth was she doing in this lonely place with this bear-like man who stood over her as though she were his victim? Then as a triumphant smile spread across his face she sprang up and leaped to her own defence.

'That makes no difference. I have a contract to do this job and I am going to do it, in spite of you or anyone else who tries to stop me.'

She thought she saw a flicker of admiration cross his face but it was soon dispelled.

'I don't want you here.'

'That's too bad, I'm staying.'

'What happened to John Sterling?'

'He has chickenpox.'

Laughter suddenly bubbled up inside her at his disgusted expression as he leaned over her.

'You'll leave tomorrow. They must send me someone else.'

'There isn't anyone else. I'm John's assistant, Ria Williams.'

She stuck out her hand, determined to get the conversation on a more businesslike footing. For a long moment, she thought he was going to ignore her hand but then he took it and held it in a most disturbing way.

'When I saw you on the boat with your camera, looking as delighted as a child on holiday I thought that's what you were, just someone on holiday,' he said, and smiled at her. 'It's no job for you. Why not admit it?'

Her foot ached to give him a kick in the shins but she smiled sweetly.

'I'm here and I'm going to do your brochure. By the time you get someone else organised, the season will be over. I understand that the job is urgent, or will next year do?'

'You know very well it's urgent. Your organisation has no business doing this to me. You'll never get it done. There are always plenty of women here with their husbands and boyfriends doing the driving because they are frightened of the mountains. What makes you think that you'll be any different?'

She clutched at the air, feeling faint and ill. He'd instinctively picked on the one thing that worried her but she stuck her chin out and looked him straight in the eye as she lied.

'I've a very good head for heights.'

'Maybe you have but you're too young. How old are you, Ria Williams? You look like a schoolgirl in that outfit.'

'I'm twenty-five years old. And how old are you, Karl Vigeland?'

The large hands shot out and landed on her shoulders.

'Don't you dare be so insolent or doesn't your firm need this job?'

She looked pointedly at each hand on her shoulder.

'Yes, it does need this job but I don't put up with this just because I am a woman.'

He removed his hands and stared at her. The silence lengthened and his expression was unreadable. Finally, when she thought she would have welcomed any comment at all from him, he spoke.

'If you stay, I want the job finished in the given time. I do not want to be bothered by you at all and neither does my staff. In other words,' he added sarcastically, 'you are on your own. Now I presume you have some kind of portfolio for me to look at.'

She licked her lips nervously, not realising how vulnerable she looked in the long blue robe.

'I'll get it. It's still in the car.'

'While you're doing that, I've got to see someone in reception. I'll only be about fifteen minutes. It's not that late and I'm sure you won't mind starting work right away.'

Gasping, she looked at her own watch which showed eleven o'clock and tried not to think of the comfortable bed in the next room.

'Of course it's not too late,' she snapped.

He looked surprised and a fleeting glimpse of a smile crossed his face.

'That's settled then.'

It seemed that he reached the door in just two long strides and then it closed behind him. Ria listened to his firm tread on the boards of the porch. She felt unable to move as she thought about Karl Vigeland. He was obviously Norwegian but his English was practically perfect. He must have travelled a great deal or perhaps even been educated in England.

Karl, she said the name slowly, thinking about the large, abrupt man who was the owner of Worldwide Journeys. One thing she knew, there would be no help from him. At best, she might be given a map and a few directions but there would be no real support. She was well and truly on her own.

Checking her watch quickly she realised that five minutes had already gone. She dived into the bedroom, undoing her robe and shrugging it off as she went. Grabbing her jeans and sweater she tugged them on in record time. A quick comb through her hair and she felt more in charge of the situation. This time, he'd see how efficient she was.

By the time she opened the door to him again her portfolio was on the table and the kettle was on and two mugs ready. Briefly he glanced at her jeans and sweater and it was obvious that he guessed why she had changed. He looked at her, a taunting smile on his face and Ria thought that this was a man who would know quickly what she was thinking. She must be careful to hold back some of herself.

Without asking, she poured two mugs of coffee and handed him one. If he took sugar, she thought, it was too bad. She looked pointedly at a chair but he sank on to the couch and as her portfolio was on the table in front of it, she was forced to sit beside him. She tried casually to put just the right amount of distance between them so that they weren't actually touching.

Usually, she had no trouble dealing with men in a businesslike manner. She knew her own worth and could keep her discussions forthright and down to earth.

As he sipped his coffee, she opened her portfolio. He made no comment on any of the pictures but just let her turn them over, not even nodding when he was ready to look at the next one. His face was expressionless and she couldn't tell if he was impressed or dismissive.

She came to the final one of a beautiful scene taken in North Wales after a storm. There were mountains in the background and a full stream overflowing with so much extra water that it bounced excitedly over fallen debris and stones. The dark, stormy mood had been captured so perfectly that people said they could nearly hear the noise of the water rushing. It was her best picture. Surely now he would say something.

'You're good.'

He dragged the words out and Ria was so busy with her thoughts that at first she didn't realise that he had spoken.

'That's settled, you can stay,' he continued.

She had the ridiculous idea that she ought to thank him and then she mentally pulled herself together.

'I always intended to.'

There was a silence as he opened the portfolio and started thumbing through at speed.

'Get some paper and a pen and I'll tell you what I want.'

Trying to throw off the idea she was once again a student taking notes from a tutor, her pen scrawled as he analysed and commented on every picture, some favourably, which she noted with relief, and others which didn't meet with his approval. He put them to one side. It wasn't only the scenery itself, he explained, but the mood of Norway which he wanted to capture. He was eager to promote it as being unique compared with other mountainous countries.

As she listened, Ria realised he wasn't the kind of man you could ask anything very much unless it was business. She guessed she would still not know much about him at the end of her stay. But a little voice inside her whispered, but you'd like to know, wouldn't you? Then sensing he was watching she was suddenly embarrassed and pretended a yawn.

'You have had a long day and have done a lot of travelling,' he stated gruffly. 'I will leave you now to go to bed. Good-night, Ria Williams.'

He stood smiling, looking down at her. His smile was the most beautiful thing she had ever seen, lighting up his eyes with unexpected flecks. She got up as he moved and followed him to the door. Suddenly he turned. They were very close. His eyes were locked with hers and then without another word, he opened the door and closed it softly behind him.

She leaned back against it, listening to the pines crunching under his feet. The meeting had not gone as she had planned or even wished but she sensed there had been a slight softening of attitude towards her. In fact he had been almost friendly by the time he left.

Maybe, she hoped, as she got ready for bed, they could have a working relationship after all. She would certainly try her hardest but knew it would not be easy. From the first time she saw him, he had appeared so terribly arrogant. A strange man, who would be difficult to get to know and even more difficult to please. Ria knew that it was more important than ever to prove she was able to produce the pictures he wanted. He would demand proof she was up to the job or without any doubt he would see she was sent home, which was the last thing she wanted. She would stay and give Karl Vigeland the best work possible, whatever it cost her.

2

The clear sunshine drew her out to the balcony and she clasped the wooden rail in much the same manner as she had clasped the ferry the previous day. But today was different. A good night's sleep had left her both rested and eager to start planning her schedule. Breathing deeply, she revelled in the view.

Deciding to explore locally, she dressed in low-heeled sandals, a deep jade full cotton skirt and a paler jade sleeveless top. She grinned at herself in the mirror thinking that she looked pretty good. Just some eye make-up and a touch of lipstick completed the picture.

When the cabin was safely locked she almost skipped down the couple of steps to where the grass lay covered with sweet-smelling pine needles. The weather was perfect, her accommodation cosy and she had a job she enjoyed. There was nothing else she needed in life.

Her mood of euphoria was short-lived as, just as she turned her car into the small space in front of the reception block, she came bonnet to bonnet with the red Porsche which was turning out. Her half wave to Karl was cut short as he eased the red car forward forcing her to slam into reverse and start to back out. As soon as there was enough room, he drew alongside her and wound down his window.

Smiling, she wound down her own, expecting to hear his thanks but the smile was soon wiped from her face as she met his scowl.

'I hope you won't spend every day getting in my way like this. There's not much room down here and most people walk to reception.'

Almost lost for words she just managed to splutter, 'I'm on my way out.'

Surely he would apologise. No-one could be that rude, but it appeared that he could.

'I want to see you some time later today. I'll come up to the cabin when I can fit it in.'

'I'll probably be out. It's a lovely day and I want to explore. I've no idea what time I'll be back.'

She was tempted to add, sorry, but then she reasoned if he wanted to be so offhand, two could play at that game. Gradually, a surprised expression crossed his face as though he wasn't used to anyone answering him back.

'I'll make it late then,' he said abruptly.

The window glided up and the Porsche shot out on to the road.

Ria had rarely experienced such rudeness. She parked carefully and made her way into reception hoping that this was not an example of Norwegian drivers in general. Her eyes sparkled angrily as she thought of a few choice names she would like to call him. If he thought she was going to hang around waiting to be summoned, he'd a surprise in store. She didn't take that kind of treatment from anybody.

She chatted for a moment with the girl who had been on duty when she'd booked in the previous evening. She was pleasant and so eager to please that gradually Ria's bad temper subsided.

'Is that man always so rude?' she asked idly, looking around the walls at the posters of waterfalls and glaciers.

She was particularly interested in one glacier which was scalloped and blue, like the icing on a cake. A visit there would be a definite must and she was so intent on the picture that she hardly heard the girl reply.

'He's a very nice man and does a lot of good in the area. Sometimes his manner is quick but he is never rude.'

'Well, he's rude to me. He's absolutely impossible.'

The girl smiled blandly as though Ria was exaggerating.

'If I can help you with anything I am

here most days. My name is Britt and perhaps it is better if you do not worry Mr Vigeland. He is very busy and also important.'

She looked at Britt's calm face and for once she was lost for words and gave in. Thanking the girl, she turned away. She knew when she was beaten and obviously Karl had quite a fan club here. Gathering up guides and brochures, she thought a trip to the nearby folk museum would help her to get the feel of the area. Knowing as much as possible about a subject helped to bring the right atmosphere into her pictures.

There was a diagram showing where it was in relation to the cabin park and she followed it easily. Today the road was straight and level and almost like home except for driving on the other side. It was a pleasant journey with the late summer sun warming her arms and soon she was turning into an open area before a long, low building. The museum was almost empty and she felt conspicuous hearing her sandals against the floor as she made her way to the desk.

The man at the desk had his back to the entrance and as he turned she almost forgot why she had come. About her own age, he was classically hand-some with dark hair and perfectly-moulded features. His tan was deep and even and his long, lean body wore jeans and sweatshirt with the jaunty confi-dence of youth. She cleared her throat slightly and started to explain slowly what she wanted to see.

'It's all right. I'm part English,' he answered in a voice low and amused.

She visibly relaxed and grinned.

'That's OK then. I won't have to use hand signs although I must admit nearly everyone I've met so far speaks such good English.'

He was easy to get on with and after she had told him what she wanted to see and why, he offered to take her on a tour personally. Over an hour sped by as he showed her the old farm implements, costumes and the beautiful

Viking boat. As she gazed at it she could imagine Karl at the head, arrogant and ready to face anything!

'Have you seen enough?'

The question startled her.

'Oh, yes.'

She paused, giving herself time to come back to the present.

'Thank you so much for taking the trouble to explain everything. I hope I haven't taken up too much of your time.'

He gave a cursory glance around.

'We're not exactly rushed off our feet and even if we were I'd still be tempted to give you all my attention.'

Ria smiled warmly at the compliment thinking what a delightful young man he was with his good looks and warm, considerate personality. When he mentioned he was about to go off duty and suggested a coffee in the adjoining timbered café, she agreed readily.

'Make yourself comfortable,' he said as they entered the café area and he pulled a chair out for her. 'By the way, I'm Erik.'

She raised her eyebrows inquiringly at the Norwegian name.

'My mother was English but my father chose my name. I know it doesn't suit me, makes people think of a huge, bearded Viking.'

'I'm Ria, well, short for Victoria actually, but that doesn't suit me either. Makes people think of a prim, Victorian lady.'

'That makes us both with unsuitable names so we've got something in common already. That's a good basis for a friendship, isn't it?'

His expression was so hopeful that for a moment she was worried that he would want to take up too much of her time.

'I'm going to be pretty busy,' she said seriously, 'although I've a feeling I could do with a friend here. The only other man I've met so far seems determined to come to blows every time we meet.'

'Looking the way you do I find that very hard to believe.'

Erik had cupped his chin in his hands and was unashamedly admiring her across the table.

'This one does. He's Karl Vigeland from the cabin park and worse still, he's the head of Worldwide Journeys and I'm currently working for him.'

Erik whistled softly.

'He has got under your skin, hasn't he? Must be a brave man to get on the wrong side of any girl with your hair colour.'

'He's dreadful and I know he's going to make the whole job difficult for me. Evidently he wanted a man to do his precious brochure, although why he thinks women can't be good photographers, I don't know.'

'Hey, calm down.' Erik smiled. 'He's a bit gruff but like all Norwegians, once you get to know him, he's OK. In fact everyone thinks very highly of him around here. He's got business interests in Europe and he's made quite a bit of money, but he does a lot for the area.'

There was an easy silence as they finished their coffee and she considered what Erik had said. It was the second time that day that someone had praised him, Ria thought in confusion. She placed her empty cup down with a slight clatter.

'But I already get the feeling he dislikes me and he doesn't even know me,' she went on.

'You're English,' Erik said, casually pushing in his chair and pulling her up beside him.

'Does he hate the English?'

'Don't look so alarmed. No, he doesn't hate them, only the women.'

'Oh, thanks,' she said sarcastically. 'That makes me feel a lot better. Why doesn't he like English women?'

'I'm not quite sure. I think it was something that happened a few years back but don't worry, you'll charm him in the end.'

She stopped listening. He was telling her not to worry but that man could hold her whole future career in his hands.

Feeling guilty for not giving him her full attention she realised Erik had stopped talking and that somehow they were now outside the café.

'Now,' she said quickly, 'I've got to find the shops. I brought stuff with me but I need bread and fresh milk, things like that.'

'No problem. I'll show you. It's not far but leave your car here and we'll pick it up later.'

He guided her in the direction of an old but sturdy-looking estate vehicle.

It was fun being with Erik, she discovered. He showed her the bank and the food shops and then they browsed around places selling tourist gifts. They chatted endlessly and she discovered that he was indeed the same age as herself and had just finished studying. As his subject was history, the museum was quite a suitable fill-in until he'd found himself a permanent job.

They lunched on the most delicious

fresh fish Ria had ever tasted.

'Straight from the fiord,' Erik explained.

She looked at the classical lines of the face opposite.

'You've got awfully good bone structure, Erik.'

'Are you trying to chat me up?' he said with mock seriousness.

'No, honestly, but would you pose for me?'

'Shouldn't that be my line?'

'Don't be so old-fashioned, besides I'm the one with the camera. But would you? I'd like to do a strong head and shoulders for my portfolio.'

'OK. I never could resist a lady with a different approach. Anytime and it'll give me a perfect excuse to see you again.'

'Don't tell me you need an excuse.'

'Oh, yes. What you see before you isn't the real me. Inside I'm shy and withdrawn,' he announced with a huge grin. 'Ria,' he questioned when she didn't return the grin, 'it's Karl, isn't it?

He's really got you worried.'

She nodded as Erik went on.

'I've met him several times since I've been here and don't worry, you'll be all right. He's a good man, very sound. He's not easy to know, I'll admit, but like most Norwegians, once they make you a friend, you're a friend for life.'

'Why couldn't he be like you?'

Ria was silent trying to believe everything Erik had said.

'Does Karl live at the cabin park?' she asked after a few moments, unable to completely rid Karl from her mind.

'Not him. He's got a house about four kilometres away. I've heard it's a fantastic place. Perhaps you'll be invited,' he added teasingly.

She shuddered and pulled a face. Then looking at her watch she gasped.

'Shouldn't you be back at the museum?'

'In half an hour. Someone is standing in for me for a couple of hours so that I can show you around.'

'Oh, how did you arrange that? I

didn't see you speak to anyone else, only the girl in the café.'

'Her brother works with me so it was easy to arrange,' he added smugly.

Gathering up her shopping, they made their way to the car.

'Thanks, Erik, you've been a life-saver today. I was feeling really strange earlier, one minute excited and the next worried to death. You've helped me to get things back into perspective.'

'I'm a troll in disguise,' was his only answer and laughing like two children, they piled her purchases on the back seat.

Later, as she was driving herself up to her cabin she saw Karl, striding in the opposite direction. He barely acknow-ledged her and she wondered in some alarm if he had called on her. Then she calmed down knowing that she had every reason to be out. Her job was to go and find the most descriptive pictures to take for the brochure. There was no way she could do that sitting in the cabin waiting for him to call.

She frowned, worrying about the way he was already affecting her after meeting him for the first time yesterday.

I can't go on like this, she told herself sternly. I've got to put him out of my mind and work in my own way or the whole thing is going to flop and my career with it.

Looking at the sky, she knew that in about an hour it would be a perfect sunset. She'd managed two coffees before she judged the colours were right and then, rejecting the tripod and taking her favourite camera, she fitted a standard lens. All her attention was caught and held by the sun going down behind the mountains, casting a myriad of colours on the slopes. At last she put down the camera and blinked. The sheer beauty of it all had left her close to tears.

'It's the most beautiful place in the world.'

Somehow she wasn't surprised to see him. It was as if she'd known all along he was there. Vaguely she wondered how long he had been watching her but it didn't seem important.

'I just hope I can do it justice.'

'I was watching the concentration and care you took,' he said gruffly.

Ria smiled, her tiredness leaving her. It had sounded suspiciously like a compliment. Neither of them spoke for several minutes as they watched the last of the sun's rays together. Karl had moved nearer and a surge of affinity to him enveloped her, as though she could read his mind and hers was laid open to him. It was as though they had called a truce. Finally he spoke.

'I've come to take you to dinner.'

Her smile became a frown because that sounded less of an invitation and more like an order. She opened her mouth to refuse and then changed her mind. There was something about the evening and the glorious sunset that would have been spoiled by an argument.

'I'll just go and change.'

'No, come as you are. We don't dress up here.'

He checked his watch.

'We're booked for fifteen minutes' time.'

Inwardly she bristled. How dare he take it for granted that she would go with him, but for once his blue eyes were sincere and friendly. Feeling torn both ways, she hesitated just briefly and then turned to collect her bag.

The Porsche had that distinctive smell of expensive leather and she leaned deeply into the seat waiting for Karl to adjust his belt and start the car. His movements were deliberate and economic and his eyes flicked over her briefly to check that she was settled. He drove quickly but expertly and once on to the clear road, he casually clicked a tape into the player so that music filled the car.

'It has to be Grieg,' she stated simply. 'I wanted to see his house when I arrived in Bergen but I didn't have the time.'

He glanced across at her, then asked,

'You like music?'

'My mother teaches it.'

He was silent and she studied his hands on the wheel, large and dependable with neat, square-cut nails. They moved almost lovingly on the steering-wheel and Ria suddenly wondered what it would be like to be held by those hands. At last the notes died away.

She wasn't quite sure how they arrived at the restaurant but Karl had his hand under her arm and was guiding her to a table. Looking around she noted that although everyone was casually dressed there was an air of relaxed affluence. She compared the crisp white linen to the checked cloth of her lunch with Erik. Now she was facing Karl and knew she would have to keep a hold not only on her tongue but also her expressions.

For a moment, she almost wished that she was back with her lunchtime companion, relaxing in his easy manner and able to be herself. Erik was as he appeared with no grudges or hidden depths. With Karl she was on guard as though they were fighting an undefined battle. He was like a hard diamond with his character split into many facets and Ria was sure that she hadn't experienced half of them yet.

Thinking he was the type of man who would probably order for them both, she was surprised when he asked what she would like, going to great lengths to explain the various dishes to her. At one point, he did recommend the fish and she hid a grin thinking that two fish meals in one day would be just too much. He lifted an inquiring eyebrow and she started to tell him about her day.

'You lunched with the boy from the museum?' he asked slowly.

'He's hardly a boy. We are exactly the same age,' she stated crossly, hiding her face in the menu and hoping the atmosphere would improve.

During the meal, she managed to defuse the conversation with small talk and eventually Karl relaxed and started to tell her about his country.

He talked with a great passion, and as she looked across at him, listening to the deep, rather deliberate voice she knew that this was a man whom she could trust with her life. He would always do the right thing and never waver from a course. If she could only prove to him how wrong he was about English women he would be a pretty fantastic person.

At last they were served the dessert, pancakes which she was told were made from cream. Served with jam and sugar they melted in her mouth.

'I couldn't manage another thing and thank you, Karl. It was a wonderful meal.'

'You do not worry about dieting?' he asked teasingly, eyeing what he could see of her slim but shapely figure across the table.

She blushed and wondered why. It was a thing she almost never did.

'No, there is always too much to do, I never need to diet.'

'Another time, you must have the smorbrod for lunch. They are our open sandwiches. Normally we only have one hot meal a day, in the evening.'

She felt quite a glutton, remembering the delightful lunchtime fish and he caught her expression and smiled. His smiles were so rare that she felt privileged and wanted to take and hold it, to keep it for the times when his face was far from smiling. Chiding herself for her ridiculous notions she unsuccessfully tried to stifle a yawn.

Immediately Karl was on his feet preparing to pay the bill. She watched him make his way up the now crowded restaurant. At one table he spoke to a group of people all about his age and there was some laughter. Ria turned away but not before she had met the cold gaze of a blond woman. She was relieved when Karl returned, leading the way out of the restaurant.

As she passed the table where the blond was seated she looked straight ahead not wanting to meet that icy glance a second time. Karl did not stop to talk to the group again but lifted his hand in a salute as he went by.

She must have dozed nearly all the way back. It was only the bumping motion of the car on the rough ground around the cabins that woke her. She was leaning horribly near to the driver's seat and sat up abruptly.

'I'm sorry. I must have dropped off. It's been a long day and after all that delicious food . . . ' Her voice trailed away.

He helped her out and they stood together in the darkness. He looked at her for a long moment as though he was wondering whether or not to kiss her. Ria held her breath, not knowing what she wanted and then suddenly he turned away abruptly.

Sighing deeply, she wondered what kind of a woman would appeal to him. He would not love easily but when he did it would be for ever and again she wondered who had made him so cynical and suspicious.

3

There followed a couple of quiet days. She saw Erik just once or twice as she called in at the museum to collect information to help with her project. She saw Karl hardly at all, just the odd time when she passed reception and he was talking to Britt.

The late Norwegian summer continued and hoping to join in some organised tours, Ria drove to the small town where she'd gone with Erik that first day. The woman in the tourist office was helpful and polite but explained patiently that although the weather was beautifully warm, the holiday season was officially over and there would be no more tours.

Ria left the little office with her shoulders slumped and a sick feeling inside. If the season was officially over there would be no alternative but to drive the mountain roads herself.

As she passed reception back at the cabin park, Britt waved wildly to her and rushed out holding an envelope.

'A message from Mr Vigeland for you,' she gasped. 'I've been very worried as I could not find you and it is important.'

Ria pulled out the single sheet of note paper. Written in a large, bold hand it instructed her to be ready at eleven o'clock to drive with him to Flaum.

'Where's Flaum, Britt?' she asked.

'Not far,' she said and waved an arm airily, 'in that direction.'

'Is it over the mountain?' Ria asked quietly.

'Oh, yes, right over the top. That is the only way.'

That settled it. She may dislike Karl intensely but if anyone could drive her safely over the heights it would be him. She frowned, knowing she would have to hide her fear but surely if she gritted her teeth and kept her mind occupied she could manage it.

Frantically getting her precious equipment ready she was suddenly looking forward to the outing. She was ready by the time Karl arrived. For a moment she was afraid to face him, afraid of the effect he would have on her and then, squaring her shoulders, she stepped outside.

Greeting her briefly, he stowed away her gear and didn't speak again until they reached the ferry. He drove the car on to the waiting boat. She looked across at him inquiringly.

'We might as well stay in the car as it's only a short crossing.'

'I haven't quite got all these ferries worked out yet. There are so many. They seem to be coming and going all day.'

Pleased by her question, he started to explain that the ferry system was just an extension of the roads. When she looked puzzled he told her to think of a road interrupted by water.

'The boat just takes you across to

pick up the same road again. It's really very simple but most tourists have difficulty in grasping it.'

Having persuaded Karl to talk about his favourite subject, his country, the conversation flowed easily and they were across the fiord and driving with a rugged mountain on one side and the water on the other. Unnoticed, the road narrowed even more, but she was listening as he spoke in his slow, deliberate manner. When he turned to her, his face was relaxed and the blue eyes were smiling and showing unexpected lighter flecks.

Then Ria gasped as a turn to the right took them swinging up a steep gradient and even farther until she could look down at the tops of the houses in the village. Even though her belt was secured she clung to the sides of her seat with both hands wondering how much higher they would be going. Like a giant spiral staircase Karl held the car round bend after bend. The road fell away to nothing and then the awful drop was on her side. With the car swinging round the bends she felt as though she were hanging out in space and tensing her stomach, began to feel sick.

Sensing his glance, she tried to compose her face and managed a brief smile through gritted teeth but it was spoiled when yet another turn caused her to cower back into her seat. This time she saw his stare.

'Please,' she whispered, 'keep your eyes on the road.'

'This is nothing. It is a road I know well,' he replied casually. 'See the snow line now?'

Nodding violently, she willed him to concentrate on driving. Never, not even in her worst nightmares, had she felt so trapped and terrified. There was no way out, nowhere to turn, nowhere to go but up and ever upwards.

'Keep your eyes on the snow. Don't look down. You'll get used to it.'

Lifting her eyes to the white tops becoming nearer all the time she tried to channel her thoughts away from her fears. As she resisted the urge to glance down she felt better. The snow appeared soft and soothing and Karl had sounded quite sympathetic. Wondering if she was being too hard on him it even occurred to her that he could help conquer her fears. In fact, she'd just decided he wasn't so bad after all when he spoke.

'If you can't get used to it, you'll be no good for the job.'

Trembling with indignation, she bit back a reply. Impulsive by nature and tending to speak first and think afterwards, she managed to curb her tongue. To argue with Karl while he was driving would be stupid in the extreme. He might know the road but she could see he needed all his concentration to cope with the now more frequent twists and turns.

Inwardly seething, she brooded on the injustice of his statement. OK, she admitted she suffered from vertigo but it certainly didn't mean she was any less of a photographer. She sensed he was waiting for the outburst of her reply and she clenched her hands, forcing herself to keep quiet.

A half smile of triumph moved his lips when she didn't answer and his words hung in the silence. Closing her eyes she let her head lean back and gave in to an overpowering exhaustion. She was quite unable to cope with both him and the road. She should never have come.

'It will be better when we reach the top,' she heard him say.

'How can you say that? It's bad enough now and I know it can only get worse.'

'When we reach the top it will be flat and the road will be level without these drops that are worrying you so much.'

Pondering on this, she noticed the car had stopped climbing and was slowing to a stop. Her eyes snapped open imagining a breakdown or some other horror but they had reached the highest point of the road.

Impulsively she turned.

'It's beautiful,' she exclaimed.

'You are glad you came?' he said matter-of-factly but she was already reaching for her camera bag with her mind busily working out the best film speeds for the brightly-lit scenes.

Snatching at the door, she was surprised by the icy blast of outside air. The sun was still shining but the ground was cold and the wind caught her hair, whipping it across her face. She shivered in the sleeveless, low-necked top. Then someone was lifting her arm and pushing it through the sleeve of her thick, woollen jacket. She stood like a child, watching his expressionless face, while he wrapped her in its snug warmth.

As the last button was fastened he watched her face and smiled. His eyes never left hers as he lifted her hair to drape it over the thick cream collar. She was drowning in the tender concern in his eyes. She wanted to lean against him and feel his arms around her, holding

57

her tightly from the wind.

As statues, they stood in the high, silent world. It could have been minutes or hours that they stood unmoving and waiting. Ria didn't know who moved first. They were suddenly apart but with the air heavy with tension.

Confused and desperately needing something to concentrate on, she took her camera and swung it round. She focused on her trembling finger searching for the shutter release. She heard the click and wondered what on earth she had photographed! Her mind was a complete blank. Then in the viewfinder she saw Karl, his head thrown back, gazing at the mountains. Almost tenderly she clicked the camera and her eyes blurred with tears.

Leaving the safety of the car, she wandered off the road, scrambling to touch the snow. She walked back and gazed at Karl between the strands of hair whipping across her face hoping to find a passion in his expression to match the wild, windy landscape but his face was stiff and blank. Fighting disappointment she turned briskly to her side of the car.

'Ready to leave?'

She nodded and sank into the seat. Karl drove slowly while she looked from side to side taking in the quiet, white beauty. Then they were leaving the flat surface with the road dipping gently at first and then swinging through tight, hairpin bends. The colour drained from her cheeks as she glanced down quickly and the world tilted crazily below.

'Don't look down.'

She looked at Karl instead, becoming almost painfully aware of him, alerted to his every movement. Only as they neared the valley did she start to unwind. At last the road was flat and then ended abruptly and she presumed they had arrived in Flaum.

Casually saying he would meet her in two hours and to be sure to get some lunch, Karl left. Not minding her own company she gazed at the fairy-tale scene. On every side, the crushed green velvet of the pine-covered slopes towered over the tiny village. Several fishing boats sat on the surface of the water, the clearness of the depths throwing back their reflection in a crazy, upside-down kaleidoscope of wooden hulls and masts.

Karl and the journey were soon forgotten as she concentrated on capturing everything on film. Although the thought of the return journey filled her with apprehension when they were finally on their way it didn't seem quite so frightening. In fact she found she was actually looking down and enjoying the breathtaking views. Her fingers were clasped together on her lap and as they rounded the last bend Karl reached across and covered them with his large, warm hand.

'You did well. It wasn't so bad, was it? You should be here in the winter when we go to our mountain huts to ski.'

'Well, that's not very likely, is it?'

'You could stay in your cabin for a few weeks longer. You've probably noticed how well it is insulated. When the wood burner is lit it is very warm.'

'One night I'm going to light it just to see what it's like.'

'I might join you,' he said casually. 'I'll even bring my own wood.'

Did all this mean he wanted her to stay? Trembling, she imagined romantic evenings with Karl in the cosy, heated cabin. Then she thrust away the thoughts and tried to remember just why she was here.

Lapsing into easy silence, they continued the journey until Ria recognised the road she had travelled several times that week. She glanced at her watch, surprised at the length of time they'd spent together. The car suddenly turned into a narrow, confined lane. She sat up straighter as they passed several expensive-looking houses.

'I must stop at my home. There is something I need,' Karl explained.

The single row of houses faced the water where some boats were moored. They bumped over the unmade road and turned into a driveway where a station wagon was already parked. He helped her up steps on to a wide veranda and into a spacious hall. Not speaking, he led the way into a large, square living-room where the walls were clad with narrow, pine timbers, like her cabin. Some leather couches, which would have dwarfed most rooms, were grouped around a low table and in a corner was a music centre which must have cost a fortune.

She held her breath as she looked at the very masculine room. It was plain and elegant and shouted money. Whatever Karl's business interests were, they were certainly profitable. She now understood the reason for his supreme confidence. He was obviously a successful businessman. There was no evidence of a woman's touch in this room, she thought. It was an all-male domain.

'Are you married?'

The question was out before she thought about what she was saying. Only then did she accept how important it was for her to have the answer. Her cheeks flushed, hoping he wouldn't read her thoughts.

'No,' he said abruptly. 'Are you?'

'No,' she replied and her eyes danced as she added impishly, 'but then I'm a lot younger than you.'

'I nearly married once, years ago.'

He seemed to be reaching for the right words. Then he shrugged as though deciding not to say any more.

'And?' she encouraged.

'She didn't like my country.'

'Your country is beautiful,' she murmured spontaneously.

Unknowingly, she had raised her face to him full of sympathy and understanding. He bent towards her, his eyes never leaving her mouth. Even as she told herself to step back, his lips touched hers so gently she wondered if

63

she had imagined it.

'Perhaps you are different,' he murmured. 'Perhaps you are stronger than I think, with your independence and your career.'

Then, as though he had never intended the brief kiss to happen, he straightened up. Dreamily she watched him briskly gathering up papers. It was evident that for him the moment had passed while she still felt the warmth of his mouth and the touch of his hand on her face.

Conversation was difficult when they left, for her mind raced ahead imagining them both in the small intimacy of her cabin. She knew she hadn't imagined his tenderness even though he gave a strong impression of fighting it. When they crunched up under the pines, a tall figure uncurled itself from her veranda steps. It was Erik, obviously pleased to see her. As she grasped the car door handle she heard Karl's intake of breath.

'What's he doing here?'

For a wonderful moment, she thought he was jealous.

'I asked him to sit for me,' she said softly. 'I want a portrait of him for my portfolio. I expect he's got a free evening and just came up.'

His expression was so incredulous that Ria thought for a moment he misunderstood. The coldness was back in his face.

'I want to take his photograph, that's all.'

'Why should you want a picture of him?' he asked, once more the abrupt man she hated.

'You heard what I said, for my portfolio,' she replied, her temper rising.

'Not in my time, you don't.'

He reached across to stop her getting out of the car.

'I'm paying for this job and it doesn't include taking pictures of boys.'

'You don't own me twenty four hours a day,' she shouted and in the small confines of the car it sounded like

65

thunder. 'I'm entitled to some free time and what I do in it is my own affair. Besides,' she added, deliberately wanting to hurt and pay him back for his dictatorial attitude, 'I enjoy his company. He's fun.'

The atmosphere crackled and looking up, she met the full fury of his steely eyes glinting dangerously at her. They stared at one another like two animals lining up for a fight. Then he spoke in clipped sentences.

'Go then. Have your fun with him. Perhaps you prefer boys. Do men take you out of your depth?'

She tried to ignore the undeserved taunt and summoning up her dignity said sarcastically, 'Thank you for an interesting day. Would you care to join us for coffee?'

In answer, he leaned across and opened her door looking as though he would like to throw her out. Taking one look at his face she staggered out quickly and without another word he was gone. Realising Erik was waiting she summoned up a smile as she reached him.

'Trouble?' he queried. 'That looked quite a scene just now in the car.'

'Nothing I can't handle,' she said. 'Mr Vigeland seems to think he owns all my time. Other than that, everything is fine.'

'Don't tell me.' He laughed. 'I came at the wrong moment.'

'It's OK, Erik,' she said, suddenly unbearably depressed. 'I just don't know what has upset my boss.'

But was that true? On the whole, everything had been good between them and there was the time on the mountain top when he was so gentle. In his house she had thought for one wild moment he wanted to kiss her more passionately. How quickly the easy companionship had degenerated into childish quarrelling. Noticing Erik watching her, she grabbed his arm.

'Come on in and have a coffee and we'll get the lighting set up.'

'You're sure it's OK? I'm not

treading on anyone's toes, am I?'

'Don't be so ridiculous! How could you possibly think that?'

It was a good evening, with Erik patiently changing his expressions and the tilt of his head until she achieved just the picture she wanted.

4

Tossing and turning, Ria knew the insistent knocking was part of her dream and if she could only wake up it would stop. She propped herself up on her pillow but the noise went on, forcing her to admit there was someone banging on her door.

Checking the small travel clock she found that she had slept through until half past nine and wanting nothing better than to snuggle under the warmth of the duvet again she decided whoever was there would go away. But they didn't, and by the sound of it they didn't intend to because there was nothing hesitant about that brisk rapping.

She dragged on her wrap and belted it quickly then running her fingers through her disordered hair moved swiftly on her bare feet. Pulling her thoughts together she frowned at the figure standing there when she opened the door. A tall blonde woman gazed at her with cool pale blue eyes.

'Yes?' she queried, conscious of her dishevelled appearance.

'Are you Ria Williams, the photographer from England?'

'Yes,' she answered, trying to smile in her usual open, friendly manner.

'You take portraits of people?'

The question was asked without any sign of friendliness and was only just this side of good manners. Ria studied her early-morning visitor. She was quite tall with a shapely and rather statuesque figure. She would certainly make a fantastic model.

'Karl has sent me to you. I think you were with him yesterday.'

'Well, yes.'

There was something about the blonde that made Ria feel she ought to give a lengthy explanation but she bit back the words as she studied her more closely. Taller than herself, and dressed in an immaculate blue suit, she was one of the loveliest and at the same time one of the most unfriendly women she had ever seen. Her pale hair hung straight and flicked on to her shoulders and she looked down her narrow nose with disdain at Ria.

Trying to smooth her hair Ria opened the door wider.

'Would you like to come in?'

She knew instinctively this was someone she was going to dislike and that she was at a disadvantage standing at the door in a housecoat with untidy hair. An icy glance swept over her as though enjoying her discomfort and suddenly she realised she had seen her before — the night Karl had taken her to dinner. She had been one of the group he had acknowledged briefly. That piercing, cold gaze was not easily forgotten.

'I do not wish to come in now but to arrange for you to take my picture.'

This was difficult. Ordinarily she would have welcomed such a model but here was a woman she knew would not be satisfied with her work.

'I would love to,' she said, trying to sound sincere and knowing she had failed miserably. 'It is rather difficult. I am working for Mr Vigeland and I have a lot to do.'

She remembered the scene last night when she told him she was using Erik as a model.

'He wants me to concentrate on the project we are working on.'

A disdainful glance swept over Ria.

'It is quite all right because the portrait of myself is for Karl.'

Ria's mouth fell open as she realised this girl was warning her off and not even being subtle about it. Summoning up all her dignity she looked coolly at the woman.

'Of course, if Mr Vigeland would like your portrait as part of this assignment I shall be happy to do this for him. However, if it is not part of this job I'm afraid I shall have to refuse.'

She took a deep breath, giving her

the courage to go on.

'I'm afraid I do not work well with models of your type. I always look for a face with warmth and character.'

Momentarily, the other woman looked at a loss. Then a condescending smile flickered lightly over her lips at Ria's impetuous words.

'I have said what I came to say and make sure you remember.'

With a swirl of blonde hair, she turned on her heel and left. Ria shut the door immediately. She leaned back against it reliving the scene that had just taken place. It was unreal, like something from a melodrama. The awful thing was she knew the girl was perfectly serious.

Suddenly she needed to sit down and think. How had the blonde gained the impression that Ria was competition? It was stupid. She didn't even like Karl and if she'd had any sense she would have told the girl and that would have been enough to send her on her way happy. But was it true? Wasn't there something about him, a hidden tenderness, a glint of humour in his eyes, a sudden and unexpected kindness?

Even breakfast didn't lift her mood and she couldn't forget the scene which left her worried and depressed. Being a friendly person herself she had never been on the receiving end of such unpleasantness, particularly from someone whom she didn't know. Then she remembered Karl had been the same when they had first met.

She'd come here with such enthusiasm and high hopes but they were all getting trampled and ground underfoot. Pausing for a moment she looked around the cabin which now was so much like home and realised she was beginning to love this country of extremes with its crystal air and gentle, wooded slopes. She was even starting to accept the challenge of the snowy, craggy tops that plunged so abruptly into the cold, deep waters. It was the people that were causing her problems.

By the time she was dressed in jeans

and a shirt, the day was not quite so bright. She'd planned to go to the glacier but glancing at the sky she tried to work out what the weather was going to do and failed. However, if she called at reception, Britt might have some idea of the day ahead.

'It is not a good time for the glacier,' Britt told her. 'Perhaps tomorrow will be better but today you had better keep near to this site because I think the cloud will come down very low.'

Prowling around, only half of her mind registered what Britt was saying while the other part was still thinking about the bad start to the morning. Then inspiration hit her nudging all thoughts of the glacier from her mind.

'Did you see a tall blonde woman this morning? She came up to see me quite early.'

She composed her face trying to appear indifferent but inwardly she was more than itching to hear the reply. The other girl frowned for a moment and then her expression cleared.

'Oh, you mean Ingrid. She is special friend of Mr Vigeland and she asked me what number you were staying in. Did she find you?'

'Oh, yes, she found me. Why do you say special friend?'

'People think for a long time they will marry. They look very nice together, both tall and strong.'

Grinning at the rather quaint description Ria asked, 'And will they, marry, I mean?'

'She would like that very much and also the parents of them both live near each other in Bergen and are friends, so it would be nice for everyone.'

'Very nice,' Ria echoed bleakly.

Once outside she was annoyed to find herself trembling. It was the way the other woman had deliberately sought her out.

The hours dragged in a haze of indecision. For the first time since she arrived, she felt lonely and was tempted to see if Erik was free for lunch.

Perhaps I'll feel better after lunch,

she thought, or maybe I've got a bout of homesickness. Taking a chunk of bread, an apple and a large mug of black coffee she sat on her veranda, trying to put her thoughts in order.

By the time she finished her meal the weather had clouded over even more and Ria knew she definitely could not go to the glacier. Restless and frustrated, she decided to take the local footpath down to the fiord and picked up her camera and a jacket.

Glad to be alone she clambered easily down with her eyes watching the build-up of clouds over the water. A lively, bubbling stream crossed and re-crossed her path at random intervals.

Certain that work-wise it was going to be a wasted day she half regretted bringing her camera but suddenly she noticed the wind was raising small waves on the surface of the fiord. In the background, the now sombre mountains stood guard, their tops overhung with dark clouds becoming a paler grey on the lower slopes. It was a perfect shot. In contrast to the brilliantly-lit scenes she had taken a few days earlier, it showed a different Norway that was dark, cold and somehow strangely menacing. It was just what she wanted to add to her growing collection. It was moody, full of atmosphere and was fantastic.

At last she clambered back up the rough path arriving at the top breathless and muddy. Then she knew what she was going to do. It was the perfect night for a fire. Dangling an old grocery box in one hand she wandered around the site picking up odd pieces of fallen wood until she was staggering under the weight. Twice she replenished her load until her porch was piled with irregularly-shaped pieces of branches and twigs.

Taking a good armful of fuel she dumped it in front of the heater while she searched around for paper and matches. She kneeled by the legs of the grey cast iron monster, peering in through the door and studying it intently. It looked quite easy and, placing some screwed-up paper in the bottom, she lit it, added some small twigs and held her breath. An immediate blaze made her sigh with relief and throwing in some larger pieces of wood she shut the door and sat back on her heels admiring her handiwork. Within minutes the cabin was beautifully warm.

Feeling contented and pleased with herself she put on some soup to simmer and was soon curled up, sipping from a large mug. This is just what I need, she told herself as she reflected on the rather dismal day. Her face was pleasantly warm and glowing and she kicked off her shoes, her whole body relaxing in the heat which reached into every corner of the room.

Indeed she was so lost in her other world that at first she didn't hear the noise. Then her body tensed as for the second time that day there was a knocking on her door. For a moment the idea that it might be Ingrid again flashed into her brain then chiding herself for being so ridiculous she reluctantly moved to open it.

Her head swam as she looked at Karl. They stared at one another, neither of them speaking then she noticed he was holding a bundle of wood rather like another man would hold a bouquet of flowers. She raised her head questioningly.

'I said I'd bring my own fuel and it's a perfect night to show you how to light the fire.'

She searched his eyes knowing there was something else he wanted to say. She smiled gently, giving him time.

'Also, I'm sorry about last night. It was wrong of me to criticise your friends.'

Nodding, she opened the door wider inviting him in and, seeing the fire already lit, he paused and grinned.

'You are a very capable lady.'

'Help yourself to some soup,' she said and pointed to the still warm saucepan.

'I was just going to change after lighting the fire.'

Whirling round she quickly gained the bedroom where she pulled off her shirt and settled for a soft blouse of pure white. She brushed her hair, then spraying herself liberally with her favourite perfume, she looked in the mirror and saw her eyes huge and dreamy and her cheeks flushed.

'Careful,' she told the mirror image. 'You look a bit too provocative.'

His face registered surprise at her altered appearance and she thought she saw a touch of satisfaction in his eyes. For a moment, ill at ease, she watched him and tried to decide where to sit. Too close and it would seem, in the cosy room, an invitation. Too far away would look ridiculous. It was a large couch and she solved the problem by settling in the far corner and bringing up her legs, rubbing the calves, explaining her walk to the fiord.

'It's left me feeling rather stiff,' she said.

'May I rub them for you?'

His face was expressionless and she was suddenly terrified to look into his eyes. Unless she was mis-reading everything, it was all moving too fast.

'No, no, they're not too bad.'

She began to talk quickly about her day, anything but look directly at him. When she told him about her afternoon walk, her face lit up with enthusiasm as she described the photographs she had taken of the low cloud over the mountains. Her voice was low and gentle and her slim hands moved expressively until Karl could picture it in his mind's eye. Now they were able to talk easily but their eyes met frequently with a language of their own which had little to do with words.

Slowly the chemistry between them built up until Ria thought it would explode. She must diffuse the situation. She jumped quickly to her feet.

'Coffee? I mean, do you want some?'

Without waiting for a reply, she filled the kettle and set out the mugs, clattering them against each other in agitation. Trying to calm herself she slowly placed a spoonful of coffee in each. She made her actions deliberate as though playing for time and putting off the inevitable, although unsure of what it was that she feared. Without knowing he had moved, she turned and came up against a hard male chest and Karl's hands were on her shoulders pulling her to him. She could feel the comfort of his strong, warm body.

Raising her head, she read at last the desire in his eyes. It wasn't happening too quickly after all. She was ready and tentatively put her arms around his waist. He seemed to be fighting for the right words but in the end he just said her name. Then his fingers were pushing back the hair from her neck and his lips placed gentle kisses which began to trail down her throat.

Suddenly the image of Ingrid flashed across her brain. She struggled, trying to push him away.

'Karl, who is Ingrid?'

His head whipped up.

'What do you know about her?'

'Only that she was here this morning. It sounds silly but I think she was telling me to stay away from you. Only not in those words . . . and well . . . '

She couldn't go on.

'She is just a friend, an old friend. Don't let her worry you, but you, my independent English girl, will be more than a friend.'

The words were whispered and gentle but they sounded like a threat. She stiffened in his arms. Was he taking revenge for the English girl who left him or were his feelings genuine? She held his head and gazed at his face, saying quietly, 'Is it me, Karl, you are making advances to or your fiancée who left you?'

His blue eyes no longer had warm flecks but were cold and steely as fury crossed his face and suddenly she realised the enormity of her accusation. Her arms locked around his neck.

'I'm sorry,' she whispered, 'so sorry.'

The blaze from his eyes terrified her as her arms were pulled away and she was pushed roughly from him, feeling confused and rejected.

'Karl, please,' she called to him with her voice and all her body, wanting to feel the warmth of him close beside her again.

Slowly he rose to his feet.

'How dare you say such a thing?'

She gazed mutely at him. Then the words rushed out in a panic as he made for the door.

'I don't know what to think,' she said, fighting back tears. 'and Ingrid this morning, she wanted me to believe you belonged to her. She looked for me deliberately. She even asked Britt the number of my cabin.'

The staccato sentences rattled out but she could see that for all the effect they were having she might as well save her breath.

'I have told you she means nothing to me but you do not believe it and if there is no trust, there is nothing. I am

85

a man of my word. I do not lie.'

'But Britt she said she expected you two to marry. What was I to think?'

'You must think whatever you wish. It is no longer important.'

He stood there, unmoved by her words, cold and hard.

'I hate you,' she sobbed, frustrated and hurt.

But she was too late. He had gone.

5

Shifting miserably under the duvet Ria watched the early-morning light. Over and over in her mind she had gone through the previous evening. Every look, word and touch had been analysed but she still had no idea of Karl's feelings for her.

Yet there was warmth and passion in his kisses and a certain sweetness but was there caring, was there the beginnings of love? She tossed and turned but the man was a mystery and she hadn't the slightest idea of how he felt. About her own feelings there was also confusion. The intensity of her response last night had shocked her. She was beginning to love Norway but was she ready to love Karl?

Punching her pillow she wondered if he hated her now. He was a proud man and had resented deeply her question about Ingrid but surely she had a right to ask him. He had come uninvited and started to make advances towards her. Yes, she threw the offending pillow from the bed, she had every right. A one-night stand was definitely not her scene. But first the rift between them must be healed and now it was her turn to make amends.

He had come to apologise last night and if he could do it then so could she. Her mood lightened. Reaching a decision, she sprang out of bed and drew back the curtains, breathing deeply and feeling that after all it was going to be a beautiful day.

Flinging a coat over her short nightshirt she left the cabin and from the pile of wood she had carefully stacked the night before, she picked a bouquet of evenly-matched lengths. They would be her peace offering. Warming to her task, she wrote on a scrap of card, just the one word, **SORRY**. Finding a green hair ribbon she threaded it through the card and wound it around the sticks.

I'm going raving mad, she told herself as she surveyed her incongruous offering, but if I want this man I must be prepared to fight for him.

Dressed, she placed her bundle carefully and almost conspiratorially on the back seat of the car. Not stopping to chat to Britt, she drove carefully, looking for the road to Karl's house.

The Porsche was missing and when she forced herself to climb the steps there was no reply so she left her wood just outside the front door. Briefly looking around she was relieved that no-one appeared to be watching her strange behaviour and, feeling slightly embarrassed, she returned to the car and backed carefully from the drive.

Noticing that she was approaching the folk museum she had an urge to see a friendly face. The empty carpark told her that Erik couldn't possibly be busy and she left the car and went in search of him. She'd been told that so late in the season there were unlikely to be many visitors and indeed the quietness was overwhelming.

Seeing his dark head bent over some papers she stood watching and when he turned, sensing her presence, the smile she received made her feel guilty and for a moment she hoped she wasn't unconsciously using him as some light relief from Karl.

'Where can I go today?' she asked as she gave him a friendly peck on the cheek. 'I've come to pick your brains.'

'Well, madam, there is plenty to see.'

He looked at her more closely, noting the circles under her eyes and the smile that was just a little forced.

'How strong are you feeling? Are you up to something strenuous?'

'I'm a bit jaded,' she admitted. 'I didn't sleep too well but it's a beautiful day and I intend to make the most of it.'

'It so happens I can get away from here in about ten minutes, so if you feel like company . . .'

His voice trailed off uncertainly.

'That's marvellous, Eric. There's no-one I'd like better, but are you sure it will be all right?'

'Well, I'm not exactly overworked as you can see. The one and only car out there belongs to you, so, I'm at your disposal. I know the perfect place to take you. Have you got plenty of film?'

'Of course,' she answered indignantly.

'Silly question, of course you have. That's settled then.'

'But where are we going? You still haven't told me.'

'Oh, the Stave Church, of course. A quick hop on a ferry and a short drive will reveal a building in the manner of the traditional Viking ships.'

Ria drove well, more used now to the jagged outcrops of rocks at the side. She even risked a glance at Erik, wondering if she could reveal anything of yesterday. She studied him, trying to see beyond the easy smile and pleasant manner. No, there wasn't anything she could tell him but perhaps a few deftly-placed questions about her early blond visitor might solve some of the puzzle.

'I know I'm irresistible but do you think you could keep your eye on the road?' he said suddenly with a teasing smile.

'I'm sorry, it's your extraordinary good looks,' she teased. 'They go straight to a girl's head.'

'I only wish it were true.'

'I can't believe there isn't a lovely Norwegian girl somewhere for you. How about older women?' she asked dramatically. 'There was an incredible blond I saw yesterday. Britt said she was a friend of Mr Vigeland.'

Erik rose to the bait beautifully.

'Oh, the lovely Ingrid. No-one is very sure about that. They're often together because I think they have shared business interests or something but no-one knows if there is more to it but they are often invited out as a couple. I haven't been here long enough to know all the details but obviously in such a small community word gets around.'

'So do you think it is serious?'

It was difficult to say the words and she hoped he didn't notice her flushed face.

'I don't think anyone really knows.'

He looked at her warm cheeks.

'Not fancying our Mr Vigeland yourself, are you?'

Looking quickly at him she saw in relief that he was teasing her.

'Not my type,' she mumbled. 'He's not friendly enough for me. Look how he . . . '

The rest of her comment was never voiced because as they rounded a bend she gasped. At first glance she was not sure whether the strange and rather pagan building was a church or not.

'Am I really seeing this?' she asked, her eyes huge.

Ignoring Erik, she tumbled hastily from the car, leaving him to lock the doors while she climbed the small slope to get a better view of the church. He came to stand beside her.

'Simplicity itself but look how it has

stood the test of time and weather.'

'Fantastic,' she said slowly.

Erik waited patiently while she circled the building taking shots from all angles, changing lenses and film. A few people watched but so absorbed in her work, she noticed none of them and even forgot about her companion until eventually she walked towards the car looking surprised to see him.

'You'd forgotten all about me, go on admit it.'

'Yes,' she admitted ruefully. 'I'm sorry but I was concentrating so . . . '

'It's OK. I'm used to being over-looked.'

Looking at his tall, slim frame and classic good looks she couldn't understand just how she could have forgotten him. Plenty of girls would like to be in her shoes with such an attractive and easy-going escort.

For the rest of the day she made an effort to be entertaining and devoted her attention to Erik. They were so compatible, each seeming to know what the other was about to say. He was like the brother she had wanted but never had, a kind friend in strictly a platonic situation. Happy and relaxed, they arrived back at the folk museum where they separated, leaving Ria to continue her way back to the site.

The afternoon sun was still high and the tops of the mountains with their covering of snow could be clearly seen. She turned to say something and then realised the passenger seat was now empty and suddenly she was incredibly lonely, just a small, insignificant figure amongst the splendour of tall trees that stood guard in every direction.

An envelope lay just inside the door and thoughts of loneliness flew as she grabbed it, tearing the envelope in her haste to see the single sheet of paper inside. It was brief.

I'm sorry as well. Wait for me this evening. There was no signature but it needed none and she held it close to her heart, knowing he had understood.

Checking her watch, she was charged

with energy and, gathering up shampoo and conditioner, she dashed into the bathroom. As she lathered her hair her mind was busy deciding what she was going to wear. Fingers poised amongst the bubbles, she bit her lip as it dawned on her that she didn't know what they were going to do. Would he take her out for another meal or would he stay here? Rinsing off her hair she adjusted the shower and began to soap herself all over while her mind mentally discarded outfit after outfit.

Later, she checked her appearance in the bedroom mirror, noting in satisfaction that her skin was soft and glowing with just the hint of a tan on her creamy arms.

Her jade dress with its matching cropped jacket would look right wherever they went but was also casual enough for just an evening walk. The healthy flush of her cheekbones needed no blusher but she carefully applied two coats of mascara to her lashes and finished with a touch of coral lipstick.

Picking up her favourite paperback she settled herself on the balcony to wait. At last unable to sit any longer, she locked the door and wandered around the cabins listening for the snarl of the Porsche. As she came out of the trees into the clearing her heart started to thud as she saw Karl talking with Britt as he was leaving the reception area.

Although she stood perfectly still, something about her must have alerted him because his head twisted around and their eyes met and locked.

As though watching a play, Ria saw the other girl touch Karl on his arm to get his attention and then, following his line of gaze, look across and smile. The clear sound of laughter drifted across making her feel slightly uncomfortable as though she were spying. Then Karl was walking across and climbing the small slope to reach her. She stood with a dryness in her mouth that had nothing to do with fear.

Then he was at her side. Looking up

into his eyes she thought how strange that they could at times be so cold and steely but were now soft and warm with dancing flecks of amber. Together they turned and walked through the trees, still without speaking. His powerful stride lengthened leaving her slightly behind but hearing her gasp, he grasped her hand and slowed his pace pulling her up the tufted slope as though she was a child.

She looked down at their joined hands, her own much paler, tipped with pink varnish and almost hidden in his tanned fingers. Never in her life had she felt so pliable and willing to be led. She followed him blindly, aware this was where she wanted to be and uncaring where he was taking her. They reached a secluded clearing ringed by pines and taking her into his arms he cradled her head against his chest with a great sigh.

'We must talk.'

He released her and pulled her down beside him. He idly picked a blade of grass, rubbing it between his fingers.

'When you are young and badly hurt it takes time to get over things. Then years later when you think it's all forgotten, sometimes the mind remembers and the hurt starts to come back.'

Touching his hand gently she found it difficult to believe that this proud, strong man could be hurt.

'You're wrong, Karl. There are people who are true and some who are not, in every country, even here.'

'Yes, I know and I travel enough to believe it with my mind but it doesn't stop the doubts creeping in.'

Already he was making her feel guilty for misjudging him and she shivered, strangely apprehensive and worried about the power and influence of this man. She was two people, one was the old, liberated Ria but there was also another girl who wanted to cling and be loved.

I'm my own person, she tried to convince herself. I'm modern and independent and I need this man like a hole in the head but also she wanted to hear more, to be reassured and made to feel secure.

'Tell me about Ingrid,' she said gently.

She listened while he told her that having known each other for years they were often classed as a couple.

'But I've never given her any indication that there was something more and I know she dates other men. Does that answer your question?'

Lifting her head she smiled. She knew instinctively that she believed what he was saying but could she put all thoughts of the other girl to one side? Whatever he said she could bet that Ingrid had other ideas and there was no doubt that she had been very thoroughly warned off.

Did she dare to upset her further by continuing to let her friendship with Karl develop knowing she would be asking for trouble? Did she want all this when she had a job to do? Biting her lip she was half inclined to tell him that their relationship must be business only.

His fingers strayed, touching her arm and feathering their way to the side of her neck. Gently he reached out, letting the other arm snake its way tightly around her and then he was lowering them both to the ground. Fire shot through Ria and she wound her arms tightly around his neck, drawing his mouth down to where she could reach it with her own.

'Ria!'

Her name was wrung from him as he cradled her, rocking her slightly. Dazed and still wanting him, she wondered why he had stopped. Her eyes questioned him and she frowned slightly.

'Tomorrow I must go away on business for a few days. Will you come with me?'

Finding it difficult to grasp what he was saying she pulled away slightly.

'What did you say?'

'Will you come away with me tomorrow?'

'What about my job?'

Knowing this was serious, she pulled

away, struggling to sit up.

'Oh, I'll get someone else to do that. I've got other plans for you.'

She froze, not quite believing what she was hearing.

'This job means everything to me. How could you suggest such a thing?'

'Wouldn't you rather come with me?'

Incredibly, she could see he really believed she would go with him and that she would give up everything and follow. Her eyes flashed a warning as her temper came to the surface.

'I understand,' she said sweetly. 'You'd like me to give up all thoughts of making a success of your brochure. You'd be happy for me to ruin my career and everything I've worked for just to go with you and be your . . . your . . . '

'You don't understand,' he just managed to interrupt.

'I understand completely.'

Tossing back her hair she sprang to her feet.

'You don't care about me and my

career. It's of no importance to you, is it? How can you be so selfish!'

Then she found herself saying the unforgivable.

'No wonder that other girl left you.'

He got quickly to his feet, towering over her.

'How dare you say that! I thought that you were different. What a fool I have been.'

'You're not a fool, just a very selfish, egotistical man.'

'If you hate me so much, why don't you go back to England? Why stay?'

'I understand,' she said sweetly. 'You'd like me to leave. Well, I don't care what you would like. I make my own decisions and I'm staying.'

'I hope you manage the roads,' he said sarcastically, 'or will you find someone else to drive you, some other fool?'

'You've never wanted me here.'

Her voice shook with fury and she had trouble pronouncing the words.

'You never wanted a woman and

perhaps all this love-making is to put me off the job and get rid of me.'

His arm shot out but she ducked and with tears streaming down her face she ran as though being chased by a hundred demons. Karl's voice thundered after her.

'Come back! You don't understand anything.'

Why should she listen to his explanations? It was obvious what he wanted of her. She'd thought he was so different, difficult, yes, but someone she could respect. Again she heard him call and she nearly faltered but then she made herself run on relentlessly, blocking out his voice. She was nearly back at the cabin before she realised he hadn't followed and that there had been no sound of his feet crashing after her.

If only there was time to get the job done and leave before he came back but perhaps there would be if she worked hard. He hadn't actually said how long he would be away. A few days was quite a loose expression and could mean anything. It might even mean a week or more.

If she could get herself together and find the strength to concentrate on work to the exclusion of everything else, it might be possible to avoid ever seeing him again.

6

Forcing herself to eat breakfast Ria considered going back to bed for the day and staying there for ever. It was difficult to be objective when she was on an unfamiliar and slippery path and there was a terrible feeling of not being in charge of her own happiness.

Trying to jolt herself back to the real world, she had only herself to blame for becoming involved with such a man. Forlornly she remembered her high hopes and enthusiasm when she discovered that this opportunity had dropped into her lap. Now here she was mooning around like a love-sick teenager which was unfair to the agency who had confidently allowed her to come. Sliding the pile of tourist literature across, she leafed through it, looking for something requiring her full concentration, something that would leave no room for any other thoughts and would occupy her entirely. Her eye was caught by the glacier and she decided to head there today.

Entering reception, she realised that Britt was not alone. Ingrid was leaning on the counter, deep in conversation. For a brief moment she panicked and turned to go but commonsense asserted itself and, pushing aside the childish impulse, she walked calmly into the room.

Ingrid turned and for a long moment said nothing but just looked Ria up and down. When she spoke, her voice held a touch of malice.

'Here comes our photographer. I wonder where she is off to today.

'Good morning,' Ria said, forcing herself to be civil. 'I'm going to the glacier. I'm here to ask Britt about the ferry times.'

'Karl won't be driving you. He is going away.'

The words were casually said but the meaning was clear.

'I know, he told me.'

Pleased with her casual reply, she felt that she had gained a point in what was developing into a match. Ingrid recovered quickly.

'He has told everyone who works for him.'

Her glance put Ria in the category of a junior employee.

'I don't actually work for him.'

She tried to hold on to her temper but she was losing the battle.

'He is employing my agency.'

Trying not to let the woman's manner unsettle her, Ria rummaged in her bag for a notebook and, flipping through the pages, she pretended an interest that she was as far from feeling. Once she turned and met Britt's eyes which were looking embarrassed and apologetic and she half smiled, not wanting to worry the younger girl.

'You saw Karl last night?' Ingrid persisted. 'Britt said you were together.'

'And if we were?'

'And if you were, it would not matter

because I am going with him now.'

She glanced at her watch.

'I must not keep him waiting.'

She grasped the door handle triumphantly and whirled round to judge the effect of her words. She paused for a moment and then she was gone.

Stepping back as though she had been slapped, Ria experienced the humiliation of realising Karl had forgotten her so quickly. Far from being upset that she refused to go with him, he had already arranged to take someone else. Needing air, she moved towards the door, letting the cool draught revive her. Gulping in steadying breaths, she noticed that Britt was watching and managed to pull herself together.

'Did I say something wrong?' the Norwegian girl asked, looking worried. 'She asked if Mr Vigeland was here last night and I said that he looked for you. I am sorry if I caused you trouble.'

'It's OK, Britt. I just don't think she likes me.'

'She does not like many people, especially women. You are much too pretty for her to like.'

Flushing with pleasure, Ria knew she was right and that jealousy and insecurity were causing the rude behaviour of the older woman but nevertheless the unkind words rankled. Trying to put her problems to one side, she forced herself to make pleasant conversation with Britt and stayed chatting until the puzzled frown left the younger girl's face. Jotting down the ferry times she risked asking if she knew how long Karl would be away but Britt only shrugged.

'No-one ever knows. He has many business interests and sometimes he goes to France and England. I would like to be your friend, Ria,' she said shyly, her honey skin slightly flushed. 'If you need any help, please ask.'

Ria choked on the emotion caused by the friendly words.

'I will,' she answered, 'and thank you. There is one thing you can do for me.

Will you let me know when my proofs arrive? They'll be in a strong cardboard package.'

Britt looked so pleased to help that it was just too much and blindly reaching for the door, Ria was glad of her dark glasses that hid the beginning of tears. Slumping in the car, she nearly gave in and went back to the cabin but if she did, it would mean Karl and Ingrid had got the better of her and that was something she just couldn't stomach.

Lifting her head and half blinded by tears, she turned on the ignition and put the car into gear. Blinking rapidly, she signalled that she was turning right and made to pull across the road. Loud hooting brought her to her senses and remembering she was driving on the opposite side to home, she quickly braked and reversed. Shivering slightly and thinking how nearly she had caused an accident, she was more than relieved to reach the ferry.

She managed the rest of the journey driving confidently and safely. While farther along she saw the bushy tops of trees level with her wheels and knew that the edge of the road dropped away, today it didn't scare her. She guessed she was near the glacier but as she came off the main road, she was certainly not prepared for the giant blue moonscape spread before her. It was more beautiful than she'd imagined and as she gazed across the water, the sun picked out the fluted edges, holding her in the spell of its fairy-like prettiness.

After completing her pictures, her mood was back to normal for the concentration on work had pushed thoughts of Karl to one side. It would have been exaggerating to say she felt happy but she was satisfied with the job. From now on work would be her only love and she could throw herself and all her energy into getting it completed and going home.

Her heart lurched as the realisation that she didn't want to return home hit her with the force of an avalanche. Conscious of a lonely evening in front of her, she lingered a long time, wishing she could paint and capture the whole panorama on one canvas. Eventually a chill breeze had her turning the car and heading back to the ferry.

There were two or three lonely evenings during the next few days but she began to welcome them and, catching up on her sleepless nights she started to feel better and more alive. Her concentration improved and she became quite proud of her ability to drive roads which would previously have given her nightmares. The days passed gently and Ria let herself go with them, trying to relax and gather her strength.

Her one worry was waiting for the proofs. She had expected to receive the first batch well before this, but a phone call informed her there had been a hold-up and the first few films would arrive together. At last, one evening, entering the gates, she saw Brit waving and after parking carefully she dashed over to join her.

'Come, I think your proofs have arrived,' Britt said, eagerly grabbing Ria by the hand and half dragging her into reception where she pointed to a bulky cardboard envelope. 'Could I see them please?'

Britt babbled on unheard as Ria looked at the package. For days she'd imagined this moment and now it was here she was terrified to see the results of her work. Changing her weight from one foot to the other, she dithered and hesitated, not wanting to open the parcel.

This was her moment of truth, her proving time. Now she would see whether her confidence in herself was justified or terribly misplaced. Her mind ran round in circles snatching at every disaster that could have happened. What if the pictures were awful? Perhaps they were out of focus or badly lit or possibly she'd made some terrible error and all she would see was nothing.

She placed a worried hand over her

forehead and then glanced up, sensing Britt's grin. Ria looked sheepishly at her and holding up crossed fingers, gave a tight, little laugh.

'Sorry, Britt.' She smiled. 'It's just that now they're actually here, I'm a bit nervous to see them.' Then seeing the other girl's disappointed expression she added, 'I tell you what. I'll look at them on my own and then I'll come down and take you back to the cabin and you can see them. That way,' she joked, 'I can take out the bad ones.'

With a dry mouth and heart pounding, she drove slowly, continually glancing at the brown parcel. Once inside the cabin, she filled the kettle and got out a coffee mug. The situation reminded her of earlier years when she'd waited for exam results to come through the letterbox. Having both parents as teachers had been a distinct disadvantage and knowing she was expected to live up to their academic level had put pressure on her.

Slitting the top of the envelope she

held it up and let the prints cascade on to the table. Desperately rummaging through them, she gave a whoop of joy as she saw they were more than good. In colour and mood she'd captured the spirit and majesty of the scenery. Sinking down with them in her hands, she leafed through more slowly in case she'd made a mistake but, no, they were perfect, sharply focused with plenty of contrast and with a something extra that put her stamp on them.

Her hand faltered as a print dropped through her fingers on to the table. She was looking at Karl, with his head thrown back as he gazed upwards to the mountains. Remembering their drive together, tears pricked her lids once more as she recalled his gentleness that day. She could almost feel his large hands wrapping the coat around her and lifting her hair over the collar.

Possibly they were never meant to come together but to live in their different worlds always miles apart. The silence in the cabin became suddenly unbearable and deciding that this brooding wasn't doing her any good, she began to pin up the pictures so she could show them to Britt. Soon the spare bedroom was like a picture gallery.

Nothing could make her feel happier than she was at this moment, and eager now to show someone her work, she burst in on Britt, dragging her by the hand and running breathlessly and laughing with her up the slope. Panting and giggling like schoolgirls, they nearly fell into the room. Britt was quiet as she studied each one in her usual calm and studious manner.

'Ria, they are wonderful. You are so clever. How I wish that I could do something like this. Mr Vigeland will be very pleased and I'm sure it will help to sell his holidays.'

Forcing herself to behave naturally, she listened while Britt pointed out the photographs which she thought Karl would like best and although the girl was no expert, she seemed to have a good eye. As she stood in her state of euphoria, almost hugging herself with satisfaction, she noticed that Britt had returned to the portrait she had taken of Erik.

'The man from the museum. He is very nice looking,' she said and although her voice was normal, there was unusual colour in her cheeks.

'Oh, Erik,' Ria said with interest. 'Do you know him?'

'We have met a few times but he is a special friend for you perhaps?'

'No, just an ordinary friend who has been very kind to me.'

'An ordinary friend. Oh, I see.'

The relief on Britt's face so easily gave away her feelings that Ria felt she ought to warn her not to reveal so much. Then shrugging, she decided it was nothing to do with her. They were two nice young people whom she hoped would get together.

'Coffee, Britt?'

She dragged her thoughts back to the present.

'No, thank you. I must get back in case anyone comes in or telephones. I should not be away but I wanted so much to see what you had done.'

'I'll walk back with you and telephone my agency, and, Britt, if you see Erik will you let him know the pictures have arrived? He'll like to see them.'

The girl's face beamed with pleasure and Ria guessed that she would make the most of the opportunity to speak to Erik.

With these excellent pictures in her portfolio, Ria realised the future spread out before her, success but a short stop away and then her head snapped up and her mood was spoiled as she heard Britt speak.

'Mr Vigeland is back tomorrow. Your pictures arrived at the right time.'

7

Ria awoke with a lovely feeling of anticipation. For a while she lingered in the luxury of her bed knowing that if she never took another photograph in Norway it didn't matter. There were more than enough pictures for a really good brochure and anything else she took would be an added bonus.

Seated on the veranda with a mug of coffee, she wrinkled her nose as the satisfying smell wafted upwards to mingle with the sweetness of the pines. The reason for her heightened senses was not difficult to find but the awareness of it hit her like a blow. Everything revolved around the fact that Karl would be back today and perhaps she would see him.

Tipping back her chair, she admitted the depth of her love for him. Whatever his faults and however much she tried to convince herself they were incompatible, the truth was staring her in the face. Unfortunately he didn't love her as he had proved by taking Ingrid away with him. He looked upon Ria as someone fresh who would stay for a few weeks and then go from his life with no strings attached. That was not for her.

Surely, she reasoned, he would come to the site if just to check with Britt that all was well after his absence. Britt would no doubt tell him that the pictures were here.

When she eventually heard a car, it was not the Porsche but she recognised the engine note. It was Erik's battered, old car and she watched him bounding up the steps, smiling and looking eager.

'Is this the one-woman picture show?' he asked, kissing her lightly on the cheek.

'Did Britt send you?' she asked.

'Yes. She's a pretty little thing, isn't she? I'd hardly noticed her before. She's usually so shy but today she was quite enthusiastic about your photographs and most insistent that I came to see them.'

She led him to the spare bedroom and stood back to watch his reaction. He looked along the walls and the silence lengthened until Ria could contain herself no longer.

'Well, what do you think of them?'

Turning, he smiled at her worried expression.

'They're good but you know that, don't you? In fact they're more than good, they are absolutely magnificent. You've really done it, Ria. These are sensational, especially this!'

He pointed to the head and shoulders of himself.

'You honestly think they're that good?' she asked.

'They're more than just good, they're fantastic.

He picked her up and swung her around in the small room. Then the teasing note went from his voice and seeing the longing in his eyes she wished sadly that he was someone else.

'To think that I never realised what a very special, talented lady you are.'

Choking back a tear, she hugged him and they held each other until a sound from the open door made her swing round.

'Is this private or can anyone join in?'

The coldness in Karl's voice hit her like a bucket of water. He stood with the light behind him, outlining his tall, strong body and just looking at him made her weak and tongue-tied. Licking her lips, she tried to speak but the casual words of welcome, rehearsed earlier, never reached her lips as she saw the furious expression on his face.

'The first of the pictures are in here,' she stuttered like a schoolgirl.

'That's the only reason I'm here,' he said pointedly and strode across the cabin, stopping just short of where they were standing and nodding briefly to Erik, saying sarcastically, 'Whatever I am interrupting you can continue later,' and pushing past them both, he entered the room.

The friendly smile was abruptly wiped from Erik's face and seeing he was about to retaliate, Ria placed a warning finger over his mouth and pulled him unceremoniously towards the door and out to the veranda. She expected Karl to be looking at her work but he had his back to the display when she rejoined him and she knew he'd been watching her and Erik. Could he possibly be jealous?

'You aren't looking at them.'

In desperation she broke the uneasy silence. Then everything was once more normal as he gave a rather bleak smile.

'I was waiting for you to show them to me.'

He touched her upper arm lightly, causing her untold misery as she longed to turn into his arms and have them wrapped around her. Unable to bear the sensations caused by his touch, she shook off his hand and he stepped back abruptly as though she'd slapped him.

'I'm sorry, I didn't know that my touch was repulsive to you.'

His clipped tones hammered her like bullets.

'It's not that, it's just . . . '

There was no way she could go on. How could she tell him that his slightest touch drove her wild with longing?

'I understand,' he bit out. 'My touch is not welcome after Erik.'

'What on earth do you mean? Erik and I are only friends.'

Then she saw the way to keep him at arms' length.

'Well,' she forced herself to say, 'perhaps a bit more than friends. He is very amusing and easy to talk to. I like him because he is friendly and concerned for me.'

Was it her imagination or did his expression change and become slightly softer? Was a thaw taking place in this Nordic man?

'Let us look at the pictures.'

He dismissed their conversation as of no consequence. He completed his circuit of the room without a word and once again the silence was frightening. Her breath was coming in gasps. At last he turned to her.

'They will do,' he said brusquely and started to leave.

'What?' she exclaimed. 'What do you mean, they will do? They are positively the best thing I've ever done. How dare you be so disparaging about my work, you egotistical man! Don't you have any feelings or doesn't kindness come into your nature?'

He moved towards her.

'Feelings! You dare to talk to me about feelings when you go from hot to cold the moment I touch you.'

'I don't understand what you mean. Why all this fuss about touching?'

She backed away, frowning, looking up at him and unable to cope with his sudden vulnerable expression.

'I will tell you and you will be in no doubt of what I mean. You look at me and there is fire in your eyes. I can see it burning like the colour of your hair. I hear it in your voice because it becomes low and you speak more slowly. But it is not real, it is not true, because every time I touch you the fire goes out. That is what I mean when I say you go from hot to cold. You lead me to believe you want me and then you push me away. It is a game to you, a cruel game.'

Not wanting to look at his face she concentrated hard on the fabric of his shirt noting the even lines of check in the colour of the cloth.

'You are a hypocrite, Ria.'

'You dare to call me that!'

Waves of pure fury rose and she was burning all over at the injustice of it. How little he understood. From the first time she saw him on the ferry she knew he would mean something to her and he had come to mean everything. But he didn't deserve her love or her loyalty. Almost sobbing she spat the words at him.

'I suppose you think you're perfect. Well, I've got news for you. This is one girl who isn't going to fall into your arms. But,' she added sweetly, 'you've always got Ingrid.'

'Ingrid? What has she got to do with it? This is you and me, Ria. I wanted you from that first time I saw you on the boat. Well, go to Erik. He is welcome to you.'

Knowing she was about to cry she tried hard to hold on to her pride.

'Yes, Erik suits me as Ingrid suits you.'

'Ingrid is nothing to me,' he muttered, 'but does Erik want you like this?'

His mouth closed over hers firmly but gently with a kiss so sweet that she could feel her strength of will draining away. Then it was over and the warm, melting sensation was abruptly shattered and she stood swaying, completely disorientated. As her mind began to function again she risked looking up and there he was, big and splendid with arrogance in every line of his body.

She was unsure how long they stayed just looking at each other. It could have been minutes or hours, a scene from somewhere out of time. It was followed by a coldness which began in her toes and spread upwards through her body.

'How does it feel?'

The question was matter of fact and without emotion.

'How does what feel?' she managed to force out.

'When the person you want to love goes cold and pushes you away. How does it feel, Ria, because you wanted me just now. I could feel it in every movement of your body.'

Bewildered, she was unable to reply and wondered if she'd heard him correctly. Slowly she realised this was his revenge.

'You did this on purpose?' she exploded, the cold sensation now overtaken by a hot fury. 'How dare you use me for your little experiments?'

Without consciously making the decision, she watched her hand come up and land a stinging slap on the side of his face.

'Whatever I did to you, it wasn't deliberate and cruel,' she spat out.

'What was it then?'

'It was how I felt at the moment, what seemed right at that time. It's difficult to explain but one thing it certainly was not and that was deliberate. I didn't mean to hurt you.'

'I would not allow myself to be hurt by you,' he answered stiffly although there was a slight relaxing of his expression.

No, she thought sadly, to admit to being hurt would be to admit to a weakness and that would not suit Karl Vigeland.

Frowning, he stepped back and then tersely changing the subject, he said crisply, 'Your work is good and will suit my brochure very well. You have done better than I expected.'

'There's nothing to keep me here any longer now. I can go tomorrow. There's no point in staying the extra few days when my work is done.'

'It is not possible for you to go,'

he said quickly.

'Why?'

'You are not booked on the boat tomorrow.'

'I'm sure that won't be a problem, just one foot passenger. I'm not taking the car. I've arranged to leave it in Bergen so I could easily get the date changed.'

'It is still not possible.'

'Don't be so ridiculous. Why?'

'Because I might need you for something else. I may decide I want another picture, something that you haven't got.'

'What, for instance?'

'You haven't got anything of the Laplanders.'

'But they live up on the high mountains.'

'Exactly, and with your fear of heights it is the one picture you have missed out on. It would be a picture to create the special atmosphere of Norway. No reindeer and no Laps,' he finished triumphantly, 'the two things that people most want to see.'

'But,' she stuttered, 'this is the first time you've mentioned this and . . . '

'It will be arranged.'

He made the announcement whilst turning on his heel. Then he was through the door and gone.

There was no doubt in her mind that Karl had won by deliberately picking on the one thing which was missing from her photographs. He had been trying to find fault to prove that he was right and she was wrong which just about summed up their relationship. Once he had seen the quality of her work and recognised it was good he cast around for something else. The Laplanders had been brilliant, she gave him that, making it appear her fear of heights prevented her from seeing them when actually she had never given them a thought.

He said it would be arranged, but not if I have anything to do with it, she decided. There is just no way I'm making another mountain trip with him. To have him looking on while I wrestle with my vertigo would be far more than I could stand.

Looking at her moist and not-too-steady hands she resolved to start planning straight away. Gazing at her pad, she settled on a programme and first on the list was a visit to the folk museum and Erik. He was sure to point her in the right direction.

Methodically she sorted through her equipment, packing the cameras, film and an assortment of lenses that she might need. Lastly, she changed into a pair of worn jeans and a thick shirt and sweater. Leaving her bag of equipment packed and ready she picked up her keys and left the cabin.

Slowly driving past reception, she saw the Porsche nose its way out to follow her. Instead of her usual smooth gear change she fumbled and stalled the car. Scarlet-faced, she turned the key and heard a faint screeching sound but the ignition caught and she turned on to the road. Usually a good driver she was all too aware of the car behind and every glance in the mirror told her it was keeping the same distance between them. She wondered how on earth she was going to get rid of him. There were no little roads leading off the main road and even if there were, she wouldn't know them.

At last he started to signal and close the distance between them. For a moment she panicked and then relaxed as she realised they were drawing near to Karl's house. Accelerating swiftly and drawing alongside her, the window of the Porsche opened and he made signs to wind down her own window. She stepped hard on the accelerator and shot away from him. She thought she caught the words, fan belt, but then shrugged them off. The car was going OK in fact it had gone very well the whole time she was here. A glance in her mirror told her he had turned for his home and feeling satisfied that she had got the better of him for once she drove on to the museum.

Erik was disappointingly vague about finding the Laplanders.

'I just want to know how I can see them.'

'Well, they start to bring their reindeer down at this time of the year so there is a fair chance you could be lucky. They also wander around selling skins but they move quickly, sometimes over the mountains and sometimes down to a village but no-one knows exactly where they will be.'

'That doesn't seem very good odds to me,' she interrupted.

'No, but what usually happens is someone sees them and word travels around quickly. It so happens that someone told me yesterday they were seen on one of the mountain roads.'

'Then I can get to them,' she said in relief.

'Providing they haven't gone somewhere else already. They don't keep to the road you know. They are just as happy going up over a mountain range. Anyway, why the urge to see them? You don't strike me as the type to buy skins or antlers.'

'I'm not, but Karl wants a picture to complete the brochure. I've got to get a picture of them so I want to go up that mountain road you mentioned.'

'I don't think you should drive it on your own. Although it's a main road there are some nasty hairpins and it's pretty high. I'll tell you what. I've got a day free at the end of the week. I could take you up there myself.'

'Thanks, Erik, that sounds a good idea,' she mumbled, knowing she had no intention of waiting until the end of the week.

Fortunately, a family came into the museum requiring his attention and mouthing a silent goodbye she left and drove thoughtfully back to the cabin park with her mind already forming a plan. Being as casual as possible she went in to chat to Britt and managed to bring the conversation around to the nearby mountains.

'How far from here to the top of the

Jotunheimen?' she asked, mentioning the road Erik had talked of.

'I would say one hundred kilometres,' Britt said. 'It is very beautiful up there and the journey down the other side to Lom is through a particularly lovely valley. Yes, it is very nice. Are you thinking of going?'

'I don't think I could fit it in. I'm going home soon and I've got to keep my strength for the drive back to Bergen.'

Laughing, she changed the subject and by that time she hoped the mention of the mountains had been forgotten. Glancing at her watch she realised it was too late to go today but tomorrow she would make the trip.

Once her decision was made she checked the cupboard making sure there was enough food for her to take for the day. She would put in a warm jacket and scarf and wear jeans and strong shoes. Not sure what to expect, she knew she might have to leave the car and walk up on the mountain.

Her mood lifted as she planned her route for the next day. Now she had something to aim for her spirits lifted. After making a list of everything she would need, she decided to have a thoroughly lazy time for what was left of the day. Making herself a mug of soup, she picked up a paperback and settled on the veranda. It was a lovely day and she might as well make the most of it. Tomorrow was well planned and she was confident she would cope with anything that might happen.

Erik said it was a main road, so everything would be easy.

8

Next morning, the sun shone and the blue of the sky was dotted with tiny fluffs of cloud. It was a perfect day for her journey and she let the car run gently down the slope. Whatever happens, she mused, no-one can say that I'm not prepared. I've got everything but a tent.

Hoping to get past reception unseen she was annoyed to find Britt standing in the doorway, but she forced herself to smile and wave casually.

There was a considerable delay for the ferry and when it finally arrived she had trouble for as she started the engine the ominous screech she heard yesterday occurred again. A couple of men seeing her on board grimaced and pointed to the car and for a moment she panicked and wondered if she should have it checked at a garage. If it happened again, she would drive to the nearest place and get some advice.

Crossing her fingers as they docked, she started the car and this time there was no unusual sound. She bumped gently off and directly in front of her was the road to the foot of the mountain. It wound gently along the edge of the fiord, passing a couple of villages.

On the map it was clearly marked as a main road so surely it couldn't be that difficult although a little voice told her she had used this argument once before. However, she determined to go on. Now the fiord was left behind and she was driving through a delightful wooded area dotted with small farms. At last she came to the junction where the main road led up across the mountains and, strongly resisting the urge to take the other fork, she swung the car over and knew there would be no going back.

Stupidly now, before she even reached the top, she began to worry about the journey down. It would be much worse and with a dry mouth she imagined the car swinging out round the hairpins. Then what she most dreaded became reality, causing her stomach to lurch as the road became a ledge on the side of the mountain but there was no alternative but to go on and up. What would she give to be safely on level ground without the terrifying sensation of hanging out in space!

An occasional car came the other way and although there was sufficient passing room, she imagined she was only able to squeeze past them. When at last she risked looking down she caught her breath, almost paralysed with fear as the old familiar vertigo gripped her. It wasn't possible she had come so high but evidently she had because the valley was a long way down and when she gazed over the side, she was horribly drawn to the edge of the void.

Clinging to the steering-wheel she saw her knuckles tight and white against the dark leather. Willing herself to be calm she managed to keep the same pressure on the accelerator, forcing the little car onwards. Then, for absolutely no reason, she thought of Karl, remembering their trip and the way he told her to look up to the snow and never down. It was madness but she could almost feel his presence, calming and talking comfortingly to her. She looked up and even the mountain co-operated as hairpin twists gave way to a series of gentle curves that were far less alarming. As though in a dream where nothing real could hurt her she pushed steadily on.

Very soon she was beyond the tree line and coming to the snow. Height markers had been placed at intervals and as she reached twelve hundred metres she was on a high plateau, making her way over the centre of the mountain. At one side were deep, icy lakes of steely blue and beyond them were the rocky peaks of the ice fields and farther beyond were the clouds.

There was a stark, cold beauty and an atmosphere of unreality quite unlike anything she had ever experienced and she itched to capture it on film. Frequently now there were stony places to pull off the road and she eased the car over and stopped. Sighing in relief she took time to flex her arms and shoulders and as she did so she glanced at her watch and was surprised that it was well past her normal lunch time. The drive had taken much longer than she expected. How long would it take to return?

Stepping from the warmth of the car, she was hit by an icy blast and rummaged in the boot for her thick jacket. The wind whipped her hair across her eyes making it difficult to focus and she hastily tied it back with a scarf, resolving to take her pictures as quickly as possible.

When she climbed back into the car, she was anxious to be on her way. Once more there was the sickening screech as she turned on the ignition and cold terror brought beads of perspiration to her forehead as she imagined how it would be to break down in this isolated place. However, her fears were forgotten as the engine caught and she drove slowly on, up to the highest point of the road.

Cruising at a walking pace, she gazed around and in spite of the warmth of the car she shivered. She appeared to be the only person up on the plateau. Keeping her eyes open for any sight of Laplanders she nearly missed the clearing at the side of the road and pulled up abruptly. They had been here, for there was the skeleton of a wigwam and what looked like the supports for some type of trading stall. Evidently they had been selling their wares, as Erik had explained yesterday.

Another car coming up from the valley slowed beside her, the plates on the back telling her it was English.

'We've missed them again. How about you, love?'

It took Ria a minute to realise that

the bluff North Countryman was referring to the Laplanders.

'They've been here though,' she said and pointed to the poles of the wigwam. 'Do you know where they've gone?' she asked hopefully.

'We heard they went over the mountain.'

He waved an arm vaguely in the direction of a high ridge.

'No chance of catching them on this road now, more's the pity. Well, cheerio, love.'

Watching them drive off, Ria thought there was little hope of seeing the Laps today but she could take a picture of the trading site with the background of the ice fields. Yes, she mused, it should be quite striking.

Nearly an hour later, she sank into the car with relief. Reaching for the flask and a sandwich, she noticed her feet were now very cold and there was a considerable drop in temperature. Resisting the temptation to take the gentle road through the valley to Lom she turned the car back in the direction of the high plateau anxious now to make her return journey.

At least it was getting warmer which was surprising. Why was it so hot when the outside temperature must be falling? A sudden sense that all was not well with the car made her heart thud and uneasily she listened to the engine. It seemed fine. Shrugging, she turned on the radio hoping that something would interest her enough to forget her forebodings, but still the feeling persisted.

Looking at the dashboard she noticed the temperature gauge was unusually high and as she continued driving it went up at an alarming rate. Thoroughly frightened, she stopped the car and saw in relief that after a time it began to swing down. Once again she continued and once again the gauge swung crazily up, forcing her to stop and wait for it to climb down.

Twice more she started and stopped and trying to keep calm reasoned that once the road dipped and she started to descend, her troubles would be over. She knew climbing would give a high reading but had never seen it like this. For a short distance all appeared well and then the worst happened. A cloud of steam rose from under the car bonnet.

For a minute she allowed herself to believe it was a freak mountain mist which would blow away but with a sinking heart knew it was no use deceiving herself for something was very wrong with the car. No wonder the men on the ferry had pointed to it. They must have been trying to tell her but in her usual self-willed fashion she had ignored them and now . . .

She had no idea what to do. She looked wildly round as though she could conjure up help but as far as she could see, the road was deserted. Taking deep breaths, she tried to think logically. Possibly it wasn't as bad as it seemed. The first thing was to check if it was anything obvious.

It would have to be glaring her in the face, she realised, knowing that things mechanical were not her best point. Pulling hard on the hand brake she got out and looked over the vehicle. It looked quite normal and she opened the bonnet to see if anything was loose. The metal was warm against her fingers and after hesitating, she lifted it and leaned over the engine compartment.

A further cloud of steam rose and she backed off looking at the ghostly mist as though it might attack her. Closing her eyes, she again willed the whole situation to go away. It wasn't fair, she was only trying to do her job. Tears of self pity splashed on her hands. What was she trying to prove? She was totally inexperienced in this type of terrain and to cap it all, did not have a good head for heights.

The road loomed as empty above as it was below and she was utterly helpless. Now she cursed her careful plans and the secretive way she had planned her journey. If she didn't arrive back nobody would know where to look and unless someone noticed her car was missing it could be tomorrow before they realised she was in trouble.

If only she had been sensible and told someone, anyone, where she was going but here she was with a broken-down car, completely on her own where nobody would dream of looking. In the meantime her position would get worse as night came and with it the cold. Stamping her feet she cast around for a solution. There was a faint glimmer of hope as she remembered the few cars she had met. After all, it was a main road and surely a vehicle would soon come along.

Slamming the bonnet she sat in the car and pulled out the map wondering if it would be possible to walk to a telephone. It might be preferable to spending the hours of darkness marooned up here, not knowing how much the temperature would drop during the night. It was the end of the Norwegian summer and although in the valleys the weather was bright and warm it would be a different story up among the lakes and snow.

A tiny nervous giggle burst from her lips as her imagination took off and she tried to see the funny side. Someone would come and help, of course they would. She wouldn't be here long and after all she had some excellent shots of the trading area and wasn't that what being an ambitious photographer was all about, taking risks to get the right shots?

She stopped worrying or even thinking about another vehicle and concentrated on helping herself. Even if she was on a mountain, she was in no danger and besides, she had a flask of coffee and a warm jacket. Spreading out the map she scrutinised the area noting there were two or three buildings marked, the nearest about four kilometres away. That wouldn't be a problem to walk to and providing it was occupied she could telephone the hire company and tell them to come and get their vehicle.

Stuffing the map in her pocket she buttoned up her jacket against the chill and after a lingering glance at the car, set off along the road. It was more difficult than she thought. The high altitude tired her, the surface was rough and to top it all, coming her way was an ominous black cloud. It waited until she had walked about one kilometre and then it opened and water deluged in long sloping arrows. Relentlessly, they pierced every part of her until she was more wet and cold than she had ever been in her life.

She raced back, stumbling and panting, the rain almost blinding in its intensity. The car had cooled considerably in the time she had been away and was just fractionally warmer than outside. She tore off the sodden jacket and grabbing a packet of tissues tried to mop up as much as possible. Shivering with cold she sat for some time before she hit on the idea of running the engine for a while.

For three hours she sat huddled and miserable, now and again running the engine while outside the light faded and with it the hope that someone would come. The prospect of the approaching night was daunting in the extreme and although she wouldn't exactly freeze at this time of the year, she knew she was in for a cold and uncomfortable few hours.

Although it meant she couldn't reach the ignition to run the engine, she decided to make herself comfortable on the back seat. If only her jacket hadn't been soaked in the rain she could have curled up under it but as it was she found a jumper and a light, knitted cardigan. Thank goodness she had thrown in a selection of clothing this morning.

After making sure there was a drop left for the morning she treated herself to another coffee then made herself as small as possible and spread the clothing over her.

Mind over matter, she told herself

sternly. Don't think about the cold but imagine being somewhere warm and cosy.

She may have slept which left her mind sluggish and dull so that she didn't at first realise that she could hear another car. By the time she had untangled herself from the sleeves of her woollen coverings it was too late and she winced as a car door slammed, ringing into the silence of the night. Heavy footsteps came towards her and she cowered into a corner.

The idea of rescue was wonderful but her mind raced in circles showing her the vulnerability of her situation. Who was coming towards her with a heavy tread? If it wasn't a rescuer it might be a mugger or worse. Pushing herself farther into her corner she saw a dark shadow looming at her window and the door handle turned. Her hand shot out to press down the lock but it was too late and it was wrenched open.

'You stupid, stubborn, foolish woman.'

The words were clipped and the voice deep.

'Karl!' she whispered not knowing whether to crouch farther into the car or wriggle across to the doorway. 'Karl, it's you, how did you . . . '

'Do you think you know better than me,' he interrupted, 'better than someone who lives here and knows the mountains well?'

Even in her drowsy state she recognised the confidence of a man supremely sure of himself and she recognised something else — he was very, very angry.

'I told you I would arrange a visit to find the Laps and I intended bringing you myself. And I also told you the fan belt was slipping on your car.'

Wide-eyed, Ria registered that he had rarely made such a long speech and obviously it wasn't over yet.

'You've broken down on a mountain. Here, that is almost a sin. Why did you attempt it alone? You've caused us all worry to say nothing of making the journey up here to find you.'

'You came to find me?' she whispered.

'Of course, but really you deserve to be left here until the morning. That would teach you a lesson.'

'But wouldn't that defeat the object of you finding me?'

She tried to make light of the situation but her voice cracked.

'This is not a joke. It is extremely serious. What if you had left the car, wandered to the edge of a lake in the dark, or slipped on a patch of snow? What then, answer me, what then?'

His eyes flashed fire and fury.

'I'm sorry,' she stuttered softly.

'Sorry! Is that all you can say? Do you realise just what has been happening down at the site?'

She didn't answer as it was only too apparent he was going to tell her and wearily she hoped she could cope with this verbal thrashing without making a fool of herself by bursting into tears.

'I came to tell you I had arranged this

trip and Britt said you hadn't been seen all day. She said you did not stop and talk this morning which she thought unusual. When she told me you inquired about the mountains, I knew where you were. It was just the inconsiderate, stubborn sort of thing that you would do.'

'So you came to find me.'

'Not straight away. I went back to see if you were in your cabin and perhaps we were mistaken but, no, you were up here on your own.'

'Thank you,' she muttered. 'The car got hotter and hotter and eventually there was all this steam and . . . '

'Well, it's no good sitting there,' he interrupted gruffly and grabbing her hand practically pulled her from the car.

A wave of dizziness and exhaustion caused her to stumble and she swayed towards him. Strong arms caught her and shivering, she nuzzled against the warmth of his sweater.

'I didn't know what to do. I tried to

walk but then it rained and . . . '

Her voice faded as he pushed her in front of him.

'Get in the Porsche. At least it's warm in there.'

Unceremoniously, he dumped her on the passenger seat and slammed the door. Guided by the headlights she watched while he pushed her car safely on to a patch of rough ground. When he was satisfied, he locked it securely and pocketing the keys came towards her.

She realised he was inside the car when she felt his hand on her thigh.

'Those jeans are damp and we've got a long drive. Take them off. Take this rug and cover yourself, then wrap it round you.'

The rug landed on her lap.

Keeping the rug over her, she pulled off the clinging, damp jeans with difficulty. He threw them into the back of the car and she trembled as he leaned across making sure the rug was right around her securely.

'Are you ready to go down?'

His face was very near and she could feel his breath against her cheek.

Unable to speak, she nodded, but he seemed satisfied and settling back in his own seat he expertly turned the car and with the headlights full on they began the journey down.

9

Blissfully confident that she was in safe hands, the journey down held no fear for Ria. Soft fingers of mist pressed against the screen locking them in their warm, safe world. Karl was quiet, his face firm with concentration, his hands steady and sure, guiding the powerful machine with the utmost control.

Wriggling her bare legs she welcomed the touch of the rough blanket as she eased off her shoes and socks. Already the memory of the last few hours took on the aspect of a bad dream. Her moments of panic, the cold and the rain were something that happened long ago or to someone else.

'Would you like some music?' he asked without looking at her.

'If you like.'

She snuggled farther into the deep upholstery.

'Grieg?' he asked, one hand already leaving the wheel to pick up a tape.

'No.'

She swallowed, remembering the last time they were alone in a car when the music of Grieg had flowed over her senses, arousing feelings which left her helpless and vulnerable.

'Something soothing,' she said and tried to keep her voice light.

'How's this?'

There was a hint of amusement in his voice. Surely the man wasn't a thought reader! The light sounds of a current favourite group filled the car and Ria relaxed. This she could handle.

Strangely, it was the absence of motion which awoke her and the suspicion that someone was staring at her. For a moment she was confused, not knowing where she was or why and then her gaze ran over the cord-covered thighs and upwards until it locked with eyes which studied her with obvious concern.

'I thought you might like to know we

are down,' he whispered as he twisted slightly in his seat to face her. 'Are you all right? You were murmuring in your dreams.'

'Down?' she questioned, feeling fuzzy with sleep.

'Down from the mountain, where you fancied spending the night.'

She peered through the window, noticing he had pulled into the side of a road that spread mercifully flat before them. She couldn't speak as the memory of her ordeal rushed back — the way she had kept her destination a secret, the stress of the drive and her terror when the car broke down. She remembered the cold, the rain and the knowledge she was to spend the night alone on the mountain. She began to shake as everything blurred and she felt tears on her cheeks.

She blinked as a handkerchief was pressed into her hand and the restriction of the seat-belt released, then the blessed warmth of wool-clad arms came around, drawing her against him. She was past caring now what he thought. Her spirit and independence were crushed by circumstances which had whirled out of her hands. Here was another human being who cared enough to cut through her secret plans and track her down.

'I didn't think anyone would find me.'

'Of course I found you.'

He pulled her more tightly to him and she let her tears soak into the wool of his sweater. She could hear tearing sobs coming in great gasps and realised they were coming from her.

'I'm sorry,' she stuttered. 'I've never been like this before but I just didn't think anyone would come and find me.'

He ran his hand over her hair, muffling her ears so that she wasn't quite sure what he was saying. She frowned thinking it sounded like, 'I'll always find you,' but he just couldn't have said that, not to her.

'I can't find the right words. You can't imagine the relief to be here.'

'What would I tell your agency if I lost you on a mountain?' he said, lightening the mood. 'We can't afford to lose people. Think what it would do to our tourist industry.'

Hearing the humour in his voice, she knew the lovely closeness was over. Just for a moment she thought something had changed between them but she was hopelessly wrong, as usual. He had come not because he loved her but because he felt responsible for her, just as he would for anyone.

Sitting up straight she dragged up the blanket and sensing his gaze, pulled it in tightly, tucking it under until she was almost sitting on the ends. He drove on swiftly with the confidence of one who knew the route well and they covered the ground in a fraction of the time it had taken her that morning. She rubbed at the window trying to see where they were.

'You won't recognise it. We've had to go the long way round as the last ferry went long ago.'

Once more he appeared to be reading her mind and she resolved in future to keep a tight grip on her wandering thoughts, just in case.

'Is this the track to your house?'

She sat up quickly and turned to question him with her glance.

'Yes.'

'What do you mean, yes? Why are we going to your house.'

'It is better that you spend the night with someone,' he stated coolly.

'But,' she exploded, 'I can't spend the night in your house.'

'Don't be ridiculous. It is the best solution. Besides,' he added smugly, 'you're supposed to be a modern, independent, liberated woman.'

'But we will be the only two there, or is there anyone else?'

'Only you and me.'

'Just you and me?' she repeated nervously. 'But . . . but . . . '

'What are you going to do? Walk back to the site, because I certainly won't take you.'

'You know I can't walk back, it's too far,' she snapped and suddenly her temper rose spiritedly and the reckless words were wrung from her letting him know plainly what she was thinking. 'I won't stay the night with you.'

She watched his long legs unfold from the car and stride along the veranda. As the door opened, a pool of light was released into the dark night, friendly and beckoning. But she resisted its call and stayed glued to her seat. Bound up in her imaginings she didn't hear the footsteps as he returned to wrench open her door.

'Are you coming or do I have to carry you?' he barked out.

It was the delay caused by trying to keep herself covered with the blanket that seemed finally to snap his patience.

'Right,' he said, just one word and she was snatched up, still clinging to her covering and carried unceremoniously into the house.

He set her down on a large leather sofa.

'You are beautiful,' he said, softly, slowly, almost like a caress.

She raised her arms to him and it was the signal he wanted and he was beside her with his head buried in her neck.

'Ria, Ria,' he said over and over again as though the saying of it alone would release his longing.

Then she could hear nothing as his mouth found her own and he was kissing her as though he would never stop. A shaft of unease came from nowhere. It was all going too fast and she was so tired.

'Karl, I . . . '

'You are tired,' he said simply, 'and must sleep.'

Almost immediately her eyes closed and she just remembered a pillow being placed under her head but she slept fitfully wondering what would have happened if she hadn't been so exhausted.

She awoke to silence and the thought that she must get away and think. It wasn't just gratitude for rescuing her.

She was in love with Karl and must get away before he realised. He was attracted to her, that was obvious, but for her it was not enough.

Everywhere was quiet as she stealthily peeped in the room hoping to find the jeans she had discarded in the car. Eventually she found them over a chair in the hall and although they were still a bit damp she dragged them on. Of Karl there was no sign but in the kitchen she found a place set with rye bread and coffee and a note propped against a platter of cheese. The writing was large and confident like the man himself and stated that he would be back shortly and to take what she needed.

The relief was wonderful as she realised how much she dreaded meeting him and then a smile touched her lips as she saw the telephone. A call to the car hire company resulted in the promise of a replacement during the morning and then, glancing at the clock, she knew Erik would be at the museum. He would help her slip away from here.

Finding the number, she managed to get through and fortunately it was Erik who answered. Briefly she said she needed to get away before Karl returned and would explain when she saw him. Obviously intrigued, he responded to the urgency in her voice by saying he could take her to the cabin park but would have to go straight back to the museum afterwards. That suited her.

Biting her lip, she looked at Karl's note, knowing that good manners necessitated her writing something. In the end she just wrote, *Thank you and goodbye*. Tears blurred her vision as she scrawled on the reverse side of the paper. She didn't even sign her name.

Waiting for Erik, she wondered what his reaction would be seeing her in damp, crumpled jeans having obviously spent the night in Karl's bungalow. However, he accepted her explanation of the rescue with horror and sympathy and didn't question the reason why Karl took her to his home. Glossing over the fact that she wanted a lift back, she said she hadn't been in a fit state to tell Karl that her agency wanted her home for another assignment. She thought how easy it was to lie when the need arose.

He was horrified to hear her car had broken down but unfortunately had to rush back to the museum so there was no time for a full explanation.

By mid morning she had showered and packed and was feeling almost human again. The hours spent on the mountain were fading into the background. She wandered into the spare bedroom and looked at the photographs which were still pinned up and decided to leave them there rather than wrap them up and put them into reception. If there were any extra from the last couple of days they could be sent on. As she picked up her portfolio the picture of Karl gazing at the mountains dropped out and on an impulse she pinned it to the wall with the rest. She would have her own copy and perhaps he would like to have it as a parting gift.

While drinking her last cup of coffee on the porch the hire company arrived with another car and after that there was nothing more to keep her from leaving. Sniffing, she brushed back the tears as she lovingly checked every room. The cabin had been home for several weeks and she was loathe to leave and the fact that she could never return was so horribly final.

The door was locked and the key ready to leave with Britt. She turned away. There was an outsize lump in her throat as she started the car and made her way down the rutted track.

She was on her way home.

10

Saying goodbye to Britt was unexpectedly painful and she realised how she would miss the pretty young Norwegian girl with her quiet, friendly manner. Britt had been full of questions about her rescue from the mountain and made no secret that she thought it very romantic.

At last Ria could postpone the moment no longer.

'I've decided to go home,' she said as calmly as she could. 'In fact I'm going today, right away.'

'Why, Ria? I thought you were here for another few days.' Britt's voice rose in surprise and then when Ria didn't answer she added thoughtfully, 'Perhaps the breakdown on the mountain has upset you but I am sure it would not happen again.'

'It isn't only that. My work here is

finished now and there is nothing to keep me any longer.'

Nothing and no-one, she thought desperately. Karl would not worry. He would probably be glad to be rid of her. Most likely he now wished he had left her to spend the night on the mountain. Coming back to the present she realised Britt was speaking.

'And I have never seen him so worried. He kept asking where I thought you were and questioning me, trying to make me remember the last time I saw you and every word we said.'

Ria frowned.

'Sorry, I don't understand. Who are you talking about?'

'Why Mr Vigeland. I have never seen him so anxious although of course it is the first time that anyone staying here has broken down.'

That, she knew, would be the reason he was so worried. It would obviously be bad publicity for his cabin park if it was known a visitor had actually been stranded. It didn't mean he was worried about her personally for he had proved that by his own disappearance this morning.

'Poor man, he was . . . ' Britt hesitated searching for the right word. 'He was, I think you say, distraught.'

For a moment, a deep tide of happiness lapped over Ria and then she pushed it away knowing that to dream of Karl would make her more and more unhappy. From now on she must find the strength to push the memories away but the word distraught insisted on lingering in the back of her mind. In fact it was hard not to question Britt and she knew she should go before some careless word gave her feelings away. Her invitation to the girl to visit her in England was genuine and when she handed over her card with her home address Britt's eyes filled with tears.

'You are so nice, Ria,' she said in a quiet voice, 'and so clever with your career. I would very much like to go to your home and be more like you. I am not very clever at all.' She hesitated then said uncertainly, 'But perhaps if I came I would be in your way.'

'You would be very welcome and we could go to places and have a lot of fun together. You are so pretty that all the English boys would be falling over themselves to take you out. As for me being clever, that's ridiculous. I can't speak your language at all but you can speak mine beautifully.'

Impulsively she leaned forward to kiss the younger woman.

'Will Erik be going to visit you in England as well?'

Britt looked at her very directly.

'Maybe he will, in any case he is part English so he could well know a lot of people in England.'

She hesitated, seeing the uncertainty battling in Britt's face.

'He is just a friend, Britt, not really my type of man at all.'

Britt's expression cleared.

'Perhaps Mr Vigeland is more your type.

Ria swallowed trying to keep her voice normal.

'No, he isn't my type either. I've yet to meet my ideal man. In any case there is Ingrid.'

Britt nodded.

'Yes, there is always Ingrid.'

That really said it all. There would always be Ingrid, waiting for Karl or travelling with him. After a few more words and promises to write, Ria eventually waved a sad goodbye. Blinking away tears she drove out of the cabin park for the last time thinking that so much had happened in the few short weeks of her stay. She had fallen hopelessly in love with a man who appeared to be made of stone, a man who played with her emotions as and when it suited him.

Trying to think more positively she knew that on the plus side she had probably done the best work of her life and held tightly to the knowledge that her career should run smoothly from now on. She knew she would need it to fill her life until the memory of Karl faded and ceased to hurt. There was just one more person to see and fortunately this time it was far easier. Erik was certain they would meet again soon.

'You'll be back,' he said firmly. 'I can see you have been charmed by this country. It shows in your pictures and your enthusiasm to photograph every aspect of life here. In any case I may well come to England again shortly to visit my mother's relations, so I shall see you.'

He hesitated and flushed, looking very young and boyish.

'We can be friends, can't we, Ria? I know you don't feel anything more but we will stay friends.'

'Of course,' she answered and knowing she ought to say more, added, 'What on earth would I have done without you? You've helped me with my research and kept me company when I needed a friend, even posed for me,' she added with a giggle. 'What man could

176

do more than that?'

Walking with her to the car, he threw a friendly arm around her shoulders and kissed her goodbye with such obvious regret that she felt guilty he had grown so fond of her. It was ironic that Britt, Erik and herself were all emotionally drawn to someone who couldn't return their feelings and with that dismal thought she left the museum and Erik.

Saying goodbye to her friends had affected her more than she realised and she experienced a deep sense of loss. Suddenly she was completely overwhelmed and pulling over to the side of the road, she rested her head on the steering-wheel and let the tears flow unchecked.

A car drew alongside and she lifted her head as the driver stared at her curiously, obviously concerned and thinking she was ill. Somehow she forced a smile and sat up and he moved on. The little episode brought her to her senses and pride forced her to set the car back on the road and continue the journey.

Her one thought now was to reach Bergen and the boat and watch the receding coast of Norway. It was a moment she longed for and at the same time dreaded, knowing that once she left Norway it would be finally all over between her and Karl. There was no possibility she would see him again.

Driving over the mountain road, her professionalism surfaced and she stopped once or twice to photograph the waterfalls which thundered down, wide and long, looking more like vertical rivers. Then, rounding a bend, her way was blocked by a flock of goats, spread lazily across the road, dozing in the sun. Stepping carefully, she wandered among them with her camera, and managed to take some close ups, portrait fashion, of the heads of a few. Then, eventually she cruised into Bergen.

It was nearly over and as she braked at a junction, a red Porsche drove across, reminding her yet again of the man she wanted to forget. Then her heart started to beat erratically as she clutched the steering-wheel with hands suddenly damp and slippery. That tawny hair and the arrogant set of the head could only belong to one man! How could he be here?

She squeezed her eyes tightly shut but he was still there when she opened them again. Thank goodness he hadn't seen her but as the thought took shape, a hold-up forced him to stop and as if her thoughts were communicating with him, he turned and their eyes locked. Even at that distance she could feel his power. He began to wave and signal to her to stay where she was but pure panic struck and quite out of character, she began to force her way through the traffic.

There were a few good-natured calls and hooting and once more she realised what a calm race they were. Had it been back home she would have been told in no uncertain manner that her behaviour was totally unacceptable. Risking a glance over her shoulder, the traffic seemed worse than ever and her last sight of Karl was with the Porsche firmly boxed in and him watching her with an unfamiliar look of helplessness.

Knowing he was in Bergen sent her straight to the car-hire firm who painstakingly checked and received the car while she fretted and fumed expecting to see Karl drive by at any moment. At last, thoroughly exhausted and drained, she was dropped at the dock by a courtesy car and herself and her luggage deposited in a cabin. The sight of her cases neatly placed together was somehow final and throwing herself on to the narrow bunk and clutching the pillow, she determined to stay there until they were well out to sea.

A glance at her watch told her there was not much longer to go and she lay tense and miserable, waiting for the movement of the boat which would take them to the open sea. The crackling of the loudspeaker giving the warning of imminent sailing time had her up and pacing the tiny cabin with agitation. Desperately she wondered why Karl was in Bergen and a treacherous yearning to see him once more assailed her. Could he be looking for her and if so why?

Suddenly hope sprang to her heart to be quickly pushed away. It was coincidence he was here and more likely a business matter which brought him to the city. It couldn't, it really couldn't be that he was looking for her and even if he was, it was far too late. She was on the boat and would soon sail for England and that would be the end of it all.

A knock on the cabin door stopped her thoughts abruptly and as she opened it a steward asked, 'Miss Williams?'

'Yes,' she answered questioningly.

'You please come with me,' and as though expecting her to agree he stood solidly holding open the door.

'Why? Where to. I don't understand . . . ' her voice trailed off.

'Please, the purser wishes to see you before we sail. It is very important.'

Grabbing her bag, her one thought was that her passport or tickets were not in order and she would be put off and not allowed to sail. Sick with apprehension she managed to keep up with the steward as he sprinted up the stairs and along the deck. Then a door opened and she was face to face with a uniformed man she supposed was the purser. He spoke rapidly in Norwegian and she frowned, thinking surely he knew she was English, until she realised there was someone else in the room who must have been behind the door when she was bundled in.

As the hair on the back of her head began to prickle she knew who it would be even before she heard the deep tones that were speaking in an unfamiliar language. Slowly she turned, dreading to meet his eyes but he didn't even look at her.

'What's going on here?' she managed to stutter but the conversation between the two men continued and there were smiles and grins as something changed hands.

Incredibly, she was through the door and securely clamped to Karl's side as he strode purposely through the last stragglers still boarding.

'You can't do this,' she managed between gritted teeth.

'Shut up and come with me. After the trouble I've taken to find you I'm taking you somewhere where we can talk.'

'I don't want to talk.'

She tried to stand still only to be relentlessly dragged along.

'I wouldn't talk to you if you were the last man on earth.'

'You're being childish again.'

This couldn't possibly be happening. Everything was so normal, people scurrying about, the smell of the salty air and in the midst of it all she was being literally abducted. Opening her mouth she tried to speak and then gave up. It was beyond her control. Seconds later, she was off the ship and almost thrown into the Porsche with the door slammed shut beside her. The car dipped as Karl's weight joined her on the other front seat.

'I suppose you realise you're kidnapping me.'

Angry tears started from her eyes and she brushed them away wildly with a hand that shook.

'That's right.'

'But you can't.'

'Lady, I have done it,' he said smugly as he swung into the traffic.

'What did you tell the purser to get him to help you like that?'

'Oh, only that you were my fiancée and we had quarrelled.'

He appeared unaware of her horrified silence.

'He quite understood, especially as he is someone I know well.'

Panicking like a trapped animal, she had just one thought in her head and that was to escape. His voice checked her as she reached for the door handle.

'You can't get out until I let you.'

His calmness irritated her beyond all rational thought and she pummelled at his arm with angry fists.

'You can't do this! I'm a British citizen.'

'Do you want to kill us both? If you want to arrive safely, you must sit still.'

'I refuse to be abducted. This is ridiculous.'

Fuming at her helplessness she left her hands in her lap where he had placed them, knowing it was stupid to fight while he was driving but his satisfied chuckle did nothing to calm her temper.

'Where are you taking me?'

'To my parents' home.'

Oh, well, she shrugged, that didn't sound too bad. Surely his parents would not be a party to any of this and if they spoke English, she would explain and they would help her get away. She could take a hotel room and wait for the next sailing. Now her position wasn't quite so vulnerable she sat quietly while Karl drove competently and swiftly.

'Where are they?' she asked as they eventually entered a strangely quiet house.

'Away for a few days so don't bother to do anything dramatic. No-one will hear you.'

The full significance of his statement hit her.

'You mean to say that they're not here?'

She swung round to confront him and looked up a long way to a satisfied smile. It was all beyond her and she couldn't cope any longer. Her strength and energy had completely gone. She sagged against him and was instantly scooped up into his arms.

After a time she murmured, 'Karl, I don't understand what's going on. How did you find me? Why did you come after me almost kidnapping me from the boat?'

A flicker of alarm flashed across her features.

'What's happened to my cameras and all my luggage?'

'They are safe and waiting for you,' he said guiltily. 'The same purser I bribed to get you off the boat dealt with your luggage as well.'

'You bribed him?'

She felt a ridiculous urge to giggle.

'Let's just say he understood my concern for your welfare.'

'But why, Karl?'

'When you were lost on the mountain I realised at that moment that I loved you,' he said simply.

Her quick intake of breath and the expression in her eyes satisfied him and he went on more firmly.

'Up until then I wanted you desperately but you seemed so independent and then of course there was Erik.'

'I thought you hated me and I just wanted to get away and go home. I couldn't bear to see you again knowing how you felt or rather how I thought you felt.'

'It was unforgivable of me I know but at that time I was so confused. I'd sworn that I would never love another English girl and then you arrived with your lovely hair and your quick ways but you seemed more interested in your work than in me.'

'Poor Karl,' she murmured, 'but it was just as bad for me. If only we'd talked to each other instead of hiding our feelings all this would never have happened.'

'When Britt told me you had gone,' he continued, 'I thought I'd go out of my mind. I was desperate to find you before the boat sailed. I was nearly too late. You've no idea how quickly I acted.'

'And if I had sailed, what then?' she asked gently.

'I would have flown to England to ask you to marry me,' he said simply.

At last the knowledge that he loved her had found its way through her confusion and she hesitated, hugging the moment to herself. Karl loved her and wanted to marry her. The silence lengthened.

'You don't love me?' he asked. 'How could I be so mistaken?'

She reached up.

'Of course I love you, although there have been moments when I've hated you and moments when I seemed to do both, but yes, I love you, Karl.'

'But will you marry me? I want a permanent relationship, a home and children. Perhaps you don't feel ready.'

For the first time she sensed that this big, confident man was unsure of himself.

'I wouldn't ask you to give up anything. I know how much your photography means to you. In fact, there are other places my tour company want to open up and we could travel together.'

'Are you offering me a job?'

'Two jobs. My wife and my company's photographer but they go together,' he finished determinedly.

'Then I accept them both but . . . '

She hesitated teasingly.

'But what?' he asked, anxiety written all over his face.

'You don't have to offer me a job. I'd already decided that I wanted to freelance.'

'That will be useful, when we have children. You do want children?'

'Yes, Karl, I want your children.'

'Ria.'

He reached for her again and she felt his desire answer her own need.

Later, Karl told her a little about his business interests of which the travel company was just one and she realised she would have quite a wealthy husband.

'Do you mind if we settle in Norway?' he asked tentatively. 'Of course, we could go to England often to see your parents. Could you live here happily with me?'

'Oh, yes,' she answered knowing she would live anywhere with him but that was something she would keep to herself. 'I wanted to be here for the winter, to see the snow and the skiing.'

'In that case, we had better be married quickly because our winter comes early. Will you marry me as soon as it can be arranged?'

'Whenever you like, on one condition.'

'And that is?'

'That while we are here, you take me to see Grieg's house.'

'Is that all?' He laughed with relief. 'Why is that so important?'

'Perhaps one day I'll tell you,' she said, looking down at his hands, as the music surged once more into her heart.

THE END

We do
rea

Did you know that all of our titles
are available for purchase?

We publish a wide range of high
quality large print books including:
Romances, Mysteries, Classics
General Fiction
Non Fiction and Westerns

Special interest titles available in
large print are:
The Little Oxford Dictionary
Music Book, Song Book
Hymn Book, Service Book

Also available from us courtesy of
Oxford University Press:
Young Readers' Dictionary
(large print edition)
Young Readers' Thesaurus
(large print edition)

For further information or a free
brochure, please contact us at:
Ulverscroft Large Print Books Ltd.,
The Green, Bradgate Road, Anstey,
Leicester, LE7 7FU, England.
Tel: (00 44) 0116 236 4325
Fax: (00 44) 0116 234 0205